"Now what do we do?"

Annabelle asked tensely.

"We plan the wedding," Bradley told her. "I'd prefer it to be small. Maybe only immediate family. But whatever you want is fine with me."

She blinked. "You can't be serious," she blurted out, unable to believe he actually meant to go through with it.

He frowned impatiently. She was looking at him as if she thought he'd lost his mind. Well, that thought had occurred to him, too. "I don't see that we have a choice. Both our reputations are on the line."

She had to admit his reasoning was valid. But she was certain he didn't honestly want to marry her, and she had her pride. "Don't you think marriage is a little drastic?" she said, determined to offer him a way out of this.

"This situation calls for drastic measures," he replied.

Dear Reader,

August is vacation month, and no matter where you're planning to go, don't forget to take along this month's Silhouette Romance novels. They're the perfect summertime read! And even if you can't get away, you can still escape from it all for a few hours of love and adventure with Silhouette Romance books.

August continues our WRITTEN IN THE STARS series. Each month in 1992 we're proud to present a book that focuses on the hero and his astrological sign. This month we're featuring the proud, passionate Leo man in Suzanne Carey's intensely emotional *Baby Swap*.

You won't want to miss the rest of our fabulous August lineup. We have love stories by Elizabeth August, Brittany Young, Carol Grace and Carla Cassidy. As a special treat, we're introducing a talented newcomer, Sandra Paul. And in months to come, watch for Silhouette Romance novels by many more of your favorite authors, including Diana Palmer, Annette Broadrick and Marie Ferrarella.

The Silhouette Romance authors and editors love to hear from readers and we'd love to hear from *you*.

Happy reading from all of us at Silhouette!

Valerie Susan Hayward
Senior Editor

ELIZABETH AUGUST

The Wife
He Wanted

Silhouette Romance

Published by Silhouette Books New York

America's Publisher of Contemporary Romance

To my parents, Bettie and Ben—
happy 50th wedding anniversary.

SILHOUETTE BOOKS
300 E. 42nd St., New York, N.Y. 10017

THE WIFE HE WANTED

Copyright © 1992 by Elizabeth August

ISBN: 0-373-08881-7

First Silhouette Books printing August 1992

Printed in the U.S.A.

Books by Elizabeth August

Silhouette Romance

Author's Choice #554
Truck Driving Woman #590
Wild Horse Canyon #626
Something So Right #668
The Nesting Instinct #719
Joey's Father #749
Ready-Made Family #771
The Man from Natchez #790
A Small Favor #809
The Cowboy and the Chauffeur #833
Like Father, Like Son #857
The Wife He Wanted #881

ELIZABETH AUGUST

lives in Wilmington, Delaware, with her husband, Doug, and her three boys, Douglas, Benjamin and Matthew. She began writing romances soon after Matthew was born. She's always wanted to write.

Elizabeth does counted cross-stitching to keep from eating at night. It doesn't always work. "I love to bowl, but I'm not very good. I keep my team's handicap high. I like hiking in the Shenandoahs, as long as we start up the mountain so that the return trip is down rather than vice versa." She loves to go to Cape Hatteras to watch the sun rise over the ocean.

Elizabeth August has also published books under the pseudonym Betsy Page.

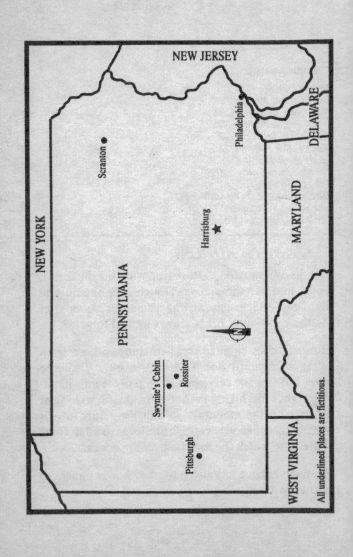

All underlined places are fictitious.

Chapter One

"P. Bradley Franklin is nobody's fool," Randall Swynite bellowed.

Annabelle Royd was glad that, at the moment at least, she was a forgotten bystander. Feigning an intense interest in the files she was arranging on the large conference table on the far side of the room, she glanced covertly at the sixty-four-year-old president and chairman of the board of Swynite Industries. He was an impressive man. Tall, standing nearly six foot four, he was a bit on the heavy side with a pouched belly that was threatening to go to flab. But even lined with age, his face was still strikingly handsome. All in all, he looked like the doyen of industry that he was, as he paced in crisp strides around the large executive office. His tastes were traditional and conservative, and Annabelle noted his slight agitation as his gaze traveled over the expensive modern decor, with its leather-and-chrome chairs and surrealistic paintings. His nose, she noted, actually wrinkled with distaste as he took in the huge marble desk that acted as a centerpiece for the room.

The younger man to whom he was speaking regarded him with cynical amusement. "You actually sound worried, Father."

Annabelle's gaze shifted to her boss, Edward Swynite. He was vice president of marketing, and this was his office. He was a younger, more slender version of his father. At forty-five, he had dark brown hair that was flecked with gray, which added a certain dignity to his appearance. And his physique appeared to have no flab or even the threat of it.

The elder Swynite stopped pacing and glared at his son. "It will take him less than a minute to realize that you have no idea how to run this company on your own."

Edward met his father's glare with a disgruntled scowl. "I am not the dunce you take me for, Father."

Annabelle silently shook her head. She had worked for Swynite Industries for seven years, the last five as Edward's administrative assistant. From her first day on the job, she'd watched these two battle. The elder Swynite was even more staunchly conservative in business matters than he was in his taste for furniture. Edward, on the other hand, had a flair for coming up with fairly extreme ideas. Some of these ideas, Annabelle felt, were quite credible, but his father would never admit to that.

Edward was seated at the marble desk. Randall came to an abrupt halt in front of it. He placed the palms of his hands flat on its cool, polished surface, then leaned forward until his face was only inches from his son's. "We will let Ann deal with Mr. Franklin. *You* will stay out of his way."

Edward continued to regard his father angrily. "I am not an incompetent lackey. I can handle this Franklin character."

"He's not interested in charm. He's only interested in the books, the nuts and bolts of running this department—something you've never greatly interested yourself in," his father pointed out curtly.

"That's for pencil pushers," Edward replied with an indifferent shrug. "I'm an idea man and I'm extraordinarily good at dealing with our customers."

"Fine. You stick to dealing with the customers," Randall growled. "Franklin is only interested in the pencil pushing aspects, so we'll let Ann deal with him. And—" Randall paused to give emphasis to what he was going to say next "—I don't want you talking to him about your ideas."

"My ideas would take this company out of the Dark Ages!" Edward snapped.

"We have a conservative board of directors. I may be its chairman, but thanks to your sister, her divorce and that vindictive husband of hers, I don't have majority control any longer. Howard Zyle proved that when he managed to push through his proposal that the president of the company has to retire at sixty-five. Luckily my position as chairman is secure. Zyle can't achieve his own goal if he uses the 'age' strategy to get me voted out. He wants that job, and since he's nearly my age, he won't try to put an age restriction on it.

However, as long as I'm alive, the other members of the board will keep me as their head. They know I built this company up from nothing, and they respect my right to retain control. And it's that same thinking that will work for you. Because I've made it clear that I've been grooming you to take my place, and they'll vote you in as president—" he leaned closer to the younger man, his eyes burning into him, willing him to do his bidding "—*unless* Franklin's report is adverse. In that case, I'm sure Howard has a hand-picked candidate for the position. So I don't want to take any chances. Franklin will be here any minute, and I want you to stay away from him."

"Fine, have it your way," Edward said, capitulating.

Annabelle had known he would give in. He always did. Everyone gave in to Randall in the end.

Suddenly Edward's attention shifted to her. "You could have tried to make yourself look a little more feminine," he admonished, his gaze raking her.

Annabelle blinked in surprise at this attack. That she sort of blended in with the furniture had never bothered him before.

"You've got nice-enough features," he continued. "You wouldn't be half bad-looking if you'd let your hair down once in a while. However, as it is, you look like a shrew with it pulled back into that tight little knot at the back of your neck. And those suits. They're expensively tailored, very professional-looking, but there isn't an ounce of femininity in them. And then there's that cool bearing of yours. When I see you moving through a room I can't help thinking of the iceberg on its way to sink the *Ti-tanic*."

Annabelle knew that Edward was upset, but that didn't give him the right to take his frustrations out on her. However, she held her own temper in check. They were all tense about this investigation of the company. She prided herself on her control, though, so she faced him with calm dignity. "Mr. Swynite, how I dress is—"

"Those four-inch high heels are the only truly feminine thing you wear," he interrupted, clearly determined not to be deterred in his critique. "But don't think you've fooled me. I know the only reason you wear them is to give yourself more height—as if you need it. You must be five foot seven in your stocking feet. And believe me, even barefooted, you could intimidate almost any man I know."

Mentally she admitted that his assessment of her appearance and bearing was correct. But it was her right to decide how she should dress and what image she would present to the world. Continuing to maintain her calm demeanor, she said, "It's the books Mr. Franklin has come to inspect, not me."

Edward continued to scowl. "It never hurts to have a pretty face smiling at a man to win his cooperation."

Annabelle felt a sudden chill as his words brought back images she had expended a great deal of energy during the past several years trying to forget. Her stomach twisted and a wave of nausea threatened. The past is past, she told herself sternly. Her muscles tensed and she pushed the ugly memories to the back of her mind. "From what I've heard of Mr. Franklin, a pretty face would not deter or influence him."

Randall was glaring at his son. "You could not find a more efficient assistant than Ann."

Annabelle had never before seen fear in the elder Swynite's eyes, but she saw a shadow of it at that moment. Was he worried that she would be so offended by Edward that she might do something vindictive, such as trying to taint Mr. Franklin's assessment of her boss? It bothered her that Randall would think her capable of such nastiness. She'd always thought she had a very open and honest relationship with these men, a relationship that would engender their trust.

She turned toward Edward and saw the same shadow of fear in his eyes. His expression changed to one of self-reproach. "I'm sorry if I offended you," he apologized. "This whole business has us all on edge."

Again she was forced to admit that his assessment of her appearance was accurate. Down deep inside, a part of her hated this image she had created for herself. But it was a defensive measure she could not give up. "No offense taken," she replied.

Edward nodded, accepting her reply but still continuing to study her speculatively. "The problem is you never smile," he said with a regretful sigh.

Her hand tightened on the paper she was holding. Now he was being really unfair. Her control slipped slightly and she scowled at him. "Of course I smile."

"All right, you never flirt," he corrected. A coaxing quality entered his voice. "Do you think that just this once, you could add a little spice to your attitude?"

Again a chill passed through her. "No," she replied firmly.

"Edward, you will allow Ann to be herself," Randall ordered, his voice carrying a distinct warning.

Edward frowned musingly, then directed his attention toward his father. "Maybe we should have Brenda help Mr. Franklin."

Annabelle expected the older Swynite to treat this suggestion as a bad joke. Instead Randall looked as if he was actually considering it. Red-hot anger swept through her. Brenda Wright was Edward's secretary. She was twenty-three, curvaceous, with long, bleached-blond hair, a cute face and an inviting giggle. Annabelle knew from the expressions on the faces of male clients that they enjoyed having Brenda around just to watch her move through a room in the tight-fitting clothing she wore. Annabelle also knew that Brenda's ability to add a bit of zest to the office atmosphere was one of the reasons Edward had hired the woman. In all fairness, Annabelle also had to admit that Brenda was an excellent secretary.

She didn't dislike Brenda. In fact, she admired the younger woman's obvious self-assuredness around men. But Annabelle did resent the suggestion that Brenda could just as easily do her job. "I was under the impression that Mr. Franklin required someone who could explain the books and the internal functioning of this department to him," she said frostily.

"Yes, yes, of course he does," the elder Swynite conceded.

Edward was smiling what Annabelle tagged his I've-just-had-an-idea-that-will-solve-the-problem smile. "You're right," he said with apology to her. "However, it won't hurt to have Brenda bring in coffee periodically."

Randall nodded. Then, turning to Annabelle, he said, "I'm counting on you to make this department look like the best run in the company." Clearly still a bit nervous about her reaction to his son's criticism, he added, "Naturally, if the department looks good, not only will Edward look good, but you will, also."

Annabelle regarded him with confidence. "You don't have to worry, sir. This is the best-run department in the company, and I intend to convince Mr. Franklin of that."

He drew a relieved breath, then smiled. "Good."

Edward grinned. "You're a treasure, Ann. And one day, if everything goes the way Dad and I want it to, you'll be running this department."

"I'd like that," she replied with open honesty. There was no sense in being coy about it. Her goal was to be a vice president at Swynite Industries, and both father and son knew it. And, unless Mr. P. Bradley Franklin threw a wrench into the proceedings, within the year, she would have achieved it.

The buzzer on Edward's desk interrupted any further discussion. "Mr. Franklin is here, sir," Brenda announced when Edward answered.

To her vexation, Annabelle experienced a sudden uneasiness in the pit of her stomach. She'd seen P. Bradley Franklin from a distance the day before. He was not quite as tall as the Swynites. She judged him to be closer to six foot two, but more muscular. His jaw was squarer. His nose was straight and fitted the rest of his features well, and his thick hair was a brownish blond. He wasn't what most women would term handsome, but he had garnered several interested looks from the women gathered at the coffee urn.

"Nice, very nice," Joan Maddenly had said, giving her appraisal in a low whisper in Annabelle's ear.

Annabelle, however, would not have used the word "nice" to describe him. Simply watching him from across the wide reception area had made her tense. Mentally she'd found herself labeling him a formidable foe. All yesterday evening and throughout the night, she'd worked on ridding herself of this notion. She'd reasoned that he was merely a man and that the marketing department was well run. There was nothing, she'd told herself a million times, to worry about.

But as he entered the office now and she got a closer look at him, he seemed even more formidable than she remembered. He did have a polite smile on his face, but it didn't quite reach those startling deep blue eyes of his that were, at this moment, scanning the occupants of the room as if taking inventory. When his scrutiny reached her, she met it with cool dignity. But that was only on the outside. To her chagrin, on the inside, she was incredibly shaky. There was an intensity in his gaze that threatened to penetrate the protective shell she kept around herself. Normally she could stare down any man. But P. Bradley Franklin wasn't just any man. This thought brought a sharp self-rebuff. *I'm overreacting because we're all so nervous about this investigation,* she reasoned. Still, feigning a sudden interest in a nearby file, she looked away from him.

"Bradley." Randall's voice was filled with welcome as he extended his hand in greeting. "Good to see you again."

"It's a pleasure to see you, too," Bradley replied.

Annabelle knew the moment his gaze left her. She suddenly found herself wishing she'd tried to talk Randall into allowing Edward to go over the books with Mr. Franklin. For one brief second, she even regretted not encouraging the idea that Brenda should do it. *You're being ridiculous!* she admonished herself.

"I'm afraid we've run into a snag," Randall was saying. "My son and I have an important meeting with some clients. Since Edward has been dealing with these people, it's very possible they will be offended if I were to show up alone. So I'm forced to take him away from you. However, this is Annabelle Royd." Pausing he waved an arm in Annabelle's direction. "She's my son's executive assistant and is totally capable of showing you the books and answering any questions you have about this particular department." He gestured toward Edward to come with him. "So if you'll excuse us?"

Edward rose with easy casualness. Smiling his most sincerely regretful smile, he rounded the desk and extended his hand toward P. Bradley Franklin. "Sorry I can't spend time with you today, but I assure you, I'm leaving you in capable hands."

Accepting the handshake, Bradley looked Edward squarely in the face. "If I have any questions Ms. Royd can't answer, I'm sure we can get together another time. I'll be here for a while."

A chill ran along Annabelle's spine. P. Bradley Franklin's voice and manner had been polite, but there had been a subtle threat and a firm statement of intent. She noticed Edward's jaw slacken slightly and knew he felt intimidated. Her shoulders straightened. Mr. Franklin might make Edward uneasy, but no man was going to cause her to quake in her shoes. At least, not visibly, she added, recalling the acutely unnerving reactions she was having every time Mr. Franklin's attention turned toward her.

It's not him, it's the situation, she told herself.

Then she saw Edward's jaw firm. She knew he didn't like feeling intimidated. It had caused a show of temper from him in the past. For a moment she tensed. But today he was clearly on his best behavior. The charm he could muster so quickly returned. "Yes, of course," he replied with a smile that suggested he would be happy to accommodate Mr. Franklin.

Drawing a relieved breath, she glanced at Randall. She saw the flicker of anxiousness in his eyes and knew he was worried that his son's pride might cause Edward to volunteer to remain. "We really have to be going," he said, his tone commanding, as he stepped aside to allow his son to pass through the door ahead of him.

Annabelle saw Edward hesitate, giving substance to Randall's concern.

"We'll be late if we don't hurry," Randall said, a look of steely determination in his eyes.

Annabelle had a sudden picture of Randall dragging Edward bodily from the room.

As if Edward had also had this same picture, he frowned resignedly. "We wouldn't want to be late," he said, and walked out.

Following Edward, Randall glanced over his shoulder and smiled with a fatherly indulgence that implied he found Bradley Franklin's presence unnecessary but was willing to tolerate it. "I'm sure Miss Royd can answer any questions you'll have, Bradley."

As the door closed, leaving her alone in the office with this tall muscular man, Annabelle experienced a wave of apprehension. Reminding herself that not only was she older and wiser than she had been eight years earlier but she was also a black belt in karate, her control returned and she faced P. Bradley Franklin with cool command.

"I've read through the salary schedules and your personnel file," he said, regarding her speculatively. "Your school records are good, not exceptional in all areas, but adequate. However, I found your salary level to be much more than adequate."

The hair on the back of her neck bristled. She wanted to tell him that what she earned was none of his business, but his mandate from the board of directors gave him the right to investigate any and all aspects of the company. "I may not have graduated at the top of my class, but I have an excellent business sense. I devote long hours to my job and have proved my worth to Mr. Swynite."

His gaze traveled over her. "He obviously values you greatly."

She heard the underlying innuendo in his voice suggesting that she was intimately involved with Edward and that her salary was a reflection of this arrangement rather than her business skills. It occurred to her that Edward would not only be stunned but appalled that P. Bradley Franklin would harbor such thoughts. She smiled dryly. "He does."

Bradley's blue eyes narrowed. "And are you prepared to prove your worth to me, Ms. Royd?"

Every muscle in her body tensed in preparation to protect herself.

He frowned impatiently. "The books, Ms. Royd?" he prodded with a nod toward the conference table.

Annabelle took a calming breath. *Get a grip on yourself.* The man might think Edward and she were an item, but he himself clearly wasn't interested in her as a woman. "I've provided all the information you requested," she said, moving toward the table.

He followed her. As she started to pull out her chair, he reached around and did it for her. "I'm from the old school," he said with an easy smile. "I seat ladies and I open doors."

The smile caused a long dimple in his left cheek, and she felt a fluttering in the pit of her stomach. That she experienced this reaction to his attempt to be charming infuriated her. He was the enemy. Besides that, he had just intimated that he thought she owed her position to her abilities in bed rather than her abilities in the office. "And I'm from the new school, Mr. Franklin. I seat myself and open my own doors," she replied.

Immediately he released her chair. "I've always believed in letting females have their own way whenever possible." With an indulgent air, he added, "They usually do, anyway."

Normally she would simply have smiled coolly at this comment that implied he considered the female sex in general to be pushy and high-handed. But Mr. P. Bradley Franklin was having a very unsettling effect upon her. "That's usually because we're right," she returned frostily.

He smiled again. "That's my mother's and my sister's claim, as well."

Immediately she wished she'd ignored his remark. She didn't want him smiling at her that way, and she didn't want to know that he had a mother and sister of whom he was clearly fond. What she wanted was to have an impersonal business relationship. She didn't know why she felt so strongly about this, and at the moment, she didn't have time to consider reasons. All she did know was that the man unnerved her.

I'm just anxious because his report means so much to my career, she reasoned. With the determination that had carried her through much more difficult times than this, she focused her attention on the papers in front of them. "Shall we begin?"

His expression became serious. "To business," he said, and seated himself.

They had barely begun, however, when Brenda entered. "Would either of you like some coffee?" she asked.

Mentally Annabelle could picture Edward on the other side of the door, his lips pursed in concentration as he listened and hoped that Brenda followed his coaching. And he won't be disappointed, Annabelle thought as the secretary stood at the door, her back straight and her shoulders held high to show off every feminine curve to its fullest.

"Yes, coffee would be nice," Bradley replied.

His indifference surprised Annabelle. She turned toward him to discover that his full attention was on the papers in front of him. He hadn't even noticed Brenda. Turning back toward the secretary, she saw Brenda regarding P. Bradley Franklin as if he presented a challenge she was determined to meet and win.

"Be back in a sec," Brenda said.

Annabelle knew that the pert secretary liked male admiration and wasn't used to being ignored. Normally Annabelle would have waited with dry amusement to see what Brenda would do to capture P. Bradley Franklin's attention. But today the possibility of the blonde's antics only irritated her.

An impatient male voice broke into her thoughts. "What do these figures represent?"

"What?" Annabelle frowned and jerked her attention back to the paper in front of P. Bradley Franklin. She couldn't believe that she was letting Brenda's behavior draw her concentration away from the business at hand. Her career had been uppermost in her mind for the past eight years. She had, in fact, made it the focus of her life. If Mr. Franklin's report went against Edward, her goals could be in serious jeopardy.

A large, strong-looking male hand was resting on a sheet of paper with columns of figures. A finger of the hand was tapping on a particular number. Quickly she read the heading of the paper, then the heading of the column. "That represents specific sales," she replied.

"Nice profit margin," he remarked, the impatience gone as he laid that page aside and started on another.

He had barely reached the bottom of the second page when Brenda returned. Annabelle had to fight to hold back a gasp. The secretary had unfastened two more buttons on her blouse, and when she leaned forward to place Mr. Franklin's coffee in front of him, so much cleavage was exposed that Annabelle was suddenly worried Brenda's ample breasts might actually escape their lacy confines and be fully bared.

"Milk or sugar or both, Mr. Franklin?" Brenda cooed, continuing to lean forward.

"Black is fine," he replied, with a polite smile.

"Would you like a doughnut?" she offered, meeting his smile with an inviting one of her own.

Annabelle's stomach unexpectedly knotted. *This is only bothering me because I don't like to see a woman flaunt herself in front of a man.* And Brenda was most definitely flaunting herself. But to Annabelle's amazement, P. Bradley Franklin didn't seem to take any notice.

"No, just the coffee," he replied dismissively.

Looking piqued, Brenda straightened. "If you want anything else, just ring," she said crisply, then strode out, her hips swinging in a seductive taunt as if to let Mr. Franklin see what he was missing.

Bradley glanced toward the door as it closed behind the secretary. "It's a wonder Mr. Swynite can get any work done."

Annabelle saw the glint of male approval in his eyes. Obviously he wasn't as immune to Brenda's charms as he'd pretended to be. But the glint was accompanied by a censorious edge in his voice. Brenda's behavior had clearly done more harm than good. Annabelle scowled. She was certain Edward had initiated the secretary's actions. One of her boss's major ploys was to find another man's weaknesses and exploit them. This time, however, the ploy had backfired. Now it was up to her to minimize the damage.

"Actually, Brenda is an excellent secretary," she said. "She types ninety words a minute without mistakes, can take dictation rapidly and correctly, has an excellent background in grammar and always checks her spelling. She's punctual and can pull out any file that's needed within seconds."

P. Bradley Franklin was regarding Annabelle with a quizzically raised eyebrow. This was the truth, but it was obvious he wasn't buying it, at least not entirely. She couldn't blame him. Brenda had behaved like the stereotypical empty-headed blond secretary who owed her job to her boss's hormones rather than her office skills. Choosing a new ploy, Annabelle decided to play on Mr. Franklin's male ego.

"Brenda is, however, used to being admired," she said. "She doesn't react well to being ignored, especially by a man she finds attractive."

Bradley looked appeased, and Annabelle mentally breathed a sigh of relief.

Suddenly a corner of his mouth tilted into a lopsided grin. "I don't embarrass too easily, but I have my limits. You don't think she'll come back in here more unbuttoned than she did this last trip, do you?"

That boyish look of his caused Annabelle's toes to want to curl with warm delight. These reactions she was having to him had her totally rattled. *What I need is a few minutes away from him,* she decided. "Why don't I just go make certain that doesn't happen," she said, rising as she spoke and moving toward the door. She was out of the room before he had a chance to respond.

Annabelle was not surprised to find Edward in the outer office. "Well, how are things going?" he asked in hushed tones.

Annabelle noted that Brenda's blouse had been rebuttoned, and she guessed from the disgruntled expression on Edward's face that he knew Brenda's mission hadn't gone as he'd hoped.

"They were going fairly well until you sent Brenda in," she said curtly.

"He's not married and, as far as I can find out, has no current steady girlfriend," Edward replied, still staring at the door of his office with a scowl. "I thought a little feminine sensuality floating around in the room might lighten his mood."

Annabelle shook her head. "I think we should stick to business." Her gaze narrowed on Edward. She wasn't in the mood to deal with any more of his unique ideas regarding the handling of Mr. Franklin. "Shouldn't you be at your club? I thought your father had arranged for you to be actually meeting with a client to back up your story to Mr. Franklin."

"Dad can handle Matin on his own," Edward replied, continuing to study the door of his office thoughtfully.

"What will you tell Mr. Franklin if he comes out and finds you here?" Annabelle asked, trying to find some way to make Edward leave before he caused any more trouble.

He shrugged. "I'll tell him that I had to come back for a file."

Annabelle glanced toward Brenda, and the blonde made a grimace that warned Annabelle that Edward would probably try something else. "What if he insists that you come in and answer a few questions?" Annabelle persisted. "He's going over the sales figures for January at the moment." This wasn't the truth, but she chose that month because she knew it would cause Edward the most concern. January sales had been down. Randall had blamed this on an ad campaign Edward had initiated. Annabelle wasn't so certain this was true; sales probably would have been slow that month, anyway. However, she knew this was a sore spot with Edward.

"January?" He frowned. "Maybe I should see how Dad and Matin are getting along."

Annabelle breathed a sigh of relief as he made a quick exit. Then she turned toward Brenda. "And please don't come in unbuttoned again."

The secretary smiled impishly. "Don't worry. I got his signal."

Annabelle started back toward the office, then stopped and returned to the secretary's desk. She told herself it wasn't any of her business, but Brenda's behavior worried her. She wondered if Brenda knew the trouble she could get herself into. "I assume Edward put you up to that, but I'm surprised you went along with it. I know you flirt with some of our clients, but it's always been rather innocent."

Brenda's grin broadened. "Most of them are flattered by a little flirting. It makes them happy. Mr. Swynite is happy if they're happy, and my job's secure."

"But what you did in there a few moments ago was more blatant than a little flirting," Annabelle pointed out.

Brenda's gaze shifted to the door of the inner office. "Mr. Swynite offered me a big bonus if I made Mr. Franklin's stay here enjoyable." Turning back toward Annabelle and reading the shock on her face, Brenda flushed. "I'm not a loose woman. Normally I would have, in polite terms, told Mr. Swynite to shove it. But—" her gaze swung back to the door of the inner office "—P. Bradley Franklin isn't married. He's wealthy, and while he's not the most handsome man I've ever seen, he's not bad-looking. The truth is, I find him attractive. All in all, if I was his type, I figured I'd come out ahead no matter what happened."

A clammy coldness spread from the top of Annabelle's head to the tip of her toes, and she felt nauseous. "You should be careful, Brenda," she warned. "You can't always predict how something might turn out."

"I suppose you're right," the blonde conceded.

I know I'm right, Annabelle confirmed mentally as she returned to the inner office.

Chapter Two

P. Bradley Franklin frowned at Annabelle. It was only fifteen minutes past five and she'd just announced that she was going home. Admittedly she'd spent a grueling day going over sales records with him, but they still weren't even half-finished. "I only have until next Wednesday to compile my report. I thought we would order dinner in and continue," he said in a voice that was more of an order than a request.

"You may stay as late as you wish," Annabelle replied, rising and then pushing her chair toward the table. "But I have another commitment. One I cannot cancel." The truth was that even if she could have canceled, she wouldn't have. She knew her attitude was ridiculous. He'd barely noticed she was a woman. Actually, he hadn't noticed that at all, she corrected wryly. Still, he made her uneasy, and she didn't want to be alone with him in a nearly empty office building.

Bradley watched her leave. Annabelle Royd was one of the coldest women he'd ever met. She hadn't smiled once all day. Might even be pretty if she did, he speculated. Her figure wasn't bad, either. In spite of the mannishly tailored suit she wore to hide it, he'd noticed that she was pleasantly rounded in all the right places. But that spinsterish, keep-your-hands-off look in her eyes would make certain no man ever got close enough for a real inspection. With a shrug, he brushed aside these observations.

Ms. Royd's personal life was none of his concern.

What did concern him though, was her nervousness. He'd noticed that from the very beginning. His gaze traveled over the papers lying on the desk. If she and the Swynites were trying to hide something from him, they were going to be sadly disappointed. Randall Swynite was chairman of the board of Swynite Industries, as well as president of the company. Edward also sat on the board because of the shares he owned. The rest of the board was composed of nine investors who owned the remainder of the shares of the company. Bradley had been hired by these board members to determine if their investment was sound, and his reputation rested on the accuracy of his assessment. Again his gaze traveled over the papers on the desk; he doubted that he would find evidence of anything disreputable or illegal here. If the Swynites, with Ms. Royd's help, were trying to hide something that he could find among the materials on this table, she would never have left him alone.

Leaning back in his chair, he stretched, reaching his arms up and slightly back while he extended his long legs forward until all the cramps were pulled out of his body. Relaxing, he continued to frown at the files and stacks of papers littering the table. Eventually he'd go through every one of them. He was a thorough man. But not tonight. He was feeling restless. He didn't usually feel restless when he was working. Apparently Ms. Royd's nervousness had affected him more than he'd thought.

He glanced toward the door and thought of Brenda. Now there was a woman who knew how to angle for a man, he mused as a lazy grin spread over his features. After her first two casts had gone badly, she'd behaved demurely, giving him no more attention than a proper secretary should. But before she'd left for the day, she'd made certain he knew where to find her.

"I'm leaving now," she'd announced, entering the office at five o'clock on the dot. "Just in case there are any files you need that you haven't asked for and you can't find, I've left my phone number on my desk. Just call. I'll be home all evening."

All the time she'd been speaking, she'd kept her full attention on Ms. Royd. But as she turned to leave, she'd given him a quick glance that let him know she would not object if he used the number for a personal call. But P. Bradley Franklin never mixed business with pleasure. Maybe when this was all over, he'd spend some time with Ms. Brenda Wright. After all, a man needed a little relaxation. For the moment, however, he had to concentrate on his investigation.

It did occur to him that secretaries generally knew more than they were credited with knowing. Brenda might have the answers he needed if he knew the right questions to ask. But at the moment he didn't even know where to begin. Squeezing his tired eyes shut, he again stretched. The image of Annabelle Royd filled his mind.

Why not? he thought. The restlessness he was feeling had put him in the mood for a challenge.

Annabelle scowled as she drove through the late-rush-hour traffic. She'd been trying to erase P. Bradley Franklin's image from her mind ever since she'd left the office, but she hadn't succeeded. A fresh rush of irritation spread through her as she recalled Brenda's final interruption. "I'm not stupid," she muttered, glancing at her image in the mirror as if needing a physical something to speak to. "I know she left that phone number for Mr. Franklin." Her scowl deepened as she again focused her gaze on the traffic. "And he knew it, too."

She wondered if, now that he was free for the evening, he might change his mind about working and take Brenda up on her unspoken invitation. This thought caused her stomach to knot, and she shot a glare at the image in the mirror. She didn't care how he spent his spare time. If he wanted to spend it with Brenda, that was fine with her. A pair of deep blue eyes mocked her. Well, she didn't! The only reason he continued to plague her was that he could adversely affect her career.

But he wouldn't be plaguing her much longer, she assured herself as she pulled into her driveway. A smile of anticipation spread over her face. Her guests this evening were guaranteed to demand all her attention and a great deal of her stamina, but she would enjoy every minute of it. Well, almost every minute, she corrected.

Bradley gave Annabelle an hour's head start. Then shoving some files into his briefcase, he left the office. Half an hour later, he was turning into her driveway in a quiet, pleasant-looking suburb on the outskirts of Pittsburgh, Pennsylvania. He didn't really expect to go over the files with her. She'd said she had other commitments for the evening. But he wanted to get a look at her away from the office. He was also interested in meeting the type of man a woman of ice would attract.

He grimaced. This curiosity wasn't like him. Why should he be interested in Annabelle Royd's private life? *I'm not,* he assured himself. *What I am interested in is why she's so edgy.*

Leaving the car, he walked up the flower-lined brick path to the front door of the two-story home. She'll probably have cats or a canary or both, he speculated, resorting to his image of the stereotypical spinster. But then it wasn't fair to think of her as a spinster, he admonished himself. She was only twenty-nine. That wasn't old.

Reaching the door, he knocked.

The sound of children squealing came from inside and he quickly glanced at the number above the door to make certain he was at the right house—1427 was there in black iron figures. That was the address he'd copied from her personnel file.

As proof, the door opened and a pair of startled mahogany brown eyes stared at him.

It was Annabelle Royd, but then it wasn't. This wasn't the woman from the office. This Ms. Royd was dressed in faded jeans with a torn knee, an old sweatshirt and sneakers that had seen better days. Most of her chestnut hair had been captured in a single pigtail that hung to several inches below her shoulders, but tendrils had escaped to frame her face in becoming disarray. And the face itself was different. It was softer, more feminine. There was a gentle look in her eyes, and laughter. *Correction*... There *had* been a gentle look mingled with laughter. Now it was gone, and a wary guardedness had taken its place.

A child's shriek suddenly jerked her attention away. "Excuse me for a minute," she said over her shoulder as she turned and rushed into the interior of the house.

For a moment, Bradley had thought that maybe Annabelle Royd had a twin sister. But the guardedness that had come over her convinced him that this was the same woman he'd spent several hours with today.

He couldn't believe he was letting his curiosity gain control of his actions, but that was exactly what was happening as he ignored her unspoken command for him to wait. Instead, he entered the house. The interior wasn't what he'd expected, either, he noted as he stood in the wide entrance hall. There were no cats, at least none lurking in view. The hall table had a clutter of mail scattered haphazardly over the surface. Three minutes ago, he'd have wagered that the very efficient Ms. Royd would have a place for everything and everything would be in its place.

An open bowl of potpourri sat in the middle of the table, its sweetly fragrant scent seeming to offer a soft welcome of its own. A memory stirred as he realized that his sister had the very same scent in her hallway. There was even a sweepstakes envelope ready to be mailed in. He would have guessed that Ms. Royd considered such things a waste of a good stamp. This house was filled with incongruities, beginning with the woman herself.

His frown deepened. The house was also filled with young children. There were now cries of distress coming from the direction in which she had headed. It sounded as if there was a whole bevy of babies in the house. Heading toward the wails, he entered a large kitchen. Three high chairs were positioned around a table occupying an alcove near a bay window, and each chair held a child. Two of the children were blond with blue eyes and looked identical. The third looked to be the same age as the others, but was dark-haired with gray eyes. Judging from his sister's kids, he guessed their ages to be somewhere near a year. The two blond babies were in tears, while the dark-haired one was watching them with an expression of silent amazement.

"I thought you liked cantaloupe," Annabelle was saying.

Bradley noticed there were a few bite-sized pieces of the fruit left on the tray belonging to the dark-haired child. The other two babies had none on their trays. Clearly, their fruit was what was now scattered all over the floor, themselves and the table. But what stunned him was the tone of Annabelle's voice. He'd expected it to be a chilly rebuke; instead, it was warm and gentle. He moved slightly to see her face. Her features were schooled into an expression of mild admonition, but from the way the corners of her mouth quivered slightly, he knew she was struggling to keep from laughing. This was not at all the woman he'd expected to find.

"Yours?" he asked, unable to think of anything else to say. According to her files, she was supposed to be both husbandless and childless. But then, people didn't always tell the truth, and maybe these three babies were the reason she was so nervous about his presence. The secret life of Annabelle Royd, he mused.

She jerked around, clearly startled to discover that he'd followed her. To his surprise he saw terror in her eyes.

Annabelle swallowed the lump of panic in her throat. His unexpected arrival in her kitchen caused her heart to seem to freeze in midmotion, then it started pounding violently. A cold sweat broke out on her palms, and her legs weakened from fear. Anger that she was letting an old terror affect her so much swept through her, giving her back her control. She faced him squarely. "They are my sister's children."

The terror had vanished almost as quickly as it had appeared, but Bradley was certain it had been there. However, at the moment, Ms. Royd's expression was one of cool reserve while her stance reminded him of a warrior prepared for hand-to-hand combat. "I didn't mean to frighten you," he apologized, then wondered if he'd been mistaken about the momentary fear he'd thought he'd seen. She certainly didn't seem like a woman who would be terrified by a mere mortal male. However, it was clear his presence was making her uneasy. "It was cold outside. I never realized that February in Pennsylvania could be so frigid." He'd also never seen a woman who could look so warm one minute and so cold the next, he added mentally. Aloud he said, "Besides, I thought you might need some help."

It irked Annabelle that she'd allowed her fear to show. "You didn't frighten me," she lied. "You merely startled me."

Suddenly Bradley was moving toward her. Immediately Annabelle braced for battle.

"Stop," he ordered with curt concern.

Realizing he wasn't even looking at her, Annabelle twisted around to discover Sarah trying to climb out of her high chair. "Sarah, sit down," she commanded, also moving toward the child.

Sarah's gaze shifted between the two adults as if appraising her chances for freedom, then slowly she sank back into her seat.

Bradley stopped a couple of feet away from the cluster of children while Annabelle examined Sarah's seat belt. "I can't understand how you always manage to get this unfastened," she fussed gently as she rebuckled it. She was trying to ignore P. Bradley Franklin's presence, but that was proving impossible. Almost like a physical touch, she could feel him watching her. "The other two seem to remain secure, but Sarah always wiggles free," she said, turning back to face him when she'd finished.

Even in her jeans, with her hair only partially caught in the loose braid and the rest hanging mussed, Annabelle gave out the silent message that she was unapproachable. *You said you were in the mood for a challenge,* he reminded himself. Besides, he didn't have a choice. He'd been hired to find out if there was any trouble at Swynite Industries, and he owed it to the people who employed him to discover what this woman was hiding—and there was no doubt in his mind that she was hiding something. "Your sister must have had all of her children close together," he replied, attempting to ease into a conversation.

"You could say that. They're triplets. Sarah and Gail are identical." Annabelle nodded toward the two blondes. Then she gently mussed the dark-haired child's hair. "Jack's the odd man out."

Bradley smiled in a comradely fashion at the boy. "Life's going to be tough for him—two sisters, and twins to boot."

The quirkish, half amused, half sorrowful smile caused a curious twinge in Annabelle's abdomen. It was almost as if she was feeling an attraction toward P. Bradley Franklin.

Immediately the protective wall of reserve she kept around herself thickened to shut out any more such reactions. "Mr. Franklin, as you can see, I have my hands full. If you'll just tell me why you're here and then be on your way, I'd be grateful."

She *did* have her hands full, Bradley admitted, but that could be to his advantage. If she was distracted, she might slip and give him a hint to what she was hiding. Then he'd know where to concentrate his probe of the company. "I've run across a few questions I'd like answered about some of the papers I've been going through," he replied.

Annabelle glanced toward the triplets. She'd fed them the cantaloupe to keep them busy until she could finish heating their dinners. Now their dinners were getting cold again, both girls were squirming, and Jack had finished his cantaloupe. That meant he'd start fussing soon. She turned back toward Bradley. "Really, Mr. Franklin, can't we go over your questions tomorrow?"

"As I told you when you left, I only have until next Wednesday to finish compiling my report," he pointed out. The very efficient Ms. Royd was looking mildly flustered. That he found her somewhat appealing at the moment shocked him.

Annabelle's jaw tensed. She could handle this. Hadn't she promised herself that she would not allow the past to rule her actions? In fact, until P. Bradley Franklin had walked into her life, she'd convinced herself that she had actually put the past behind her. She knew now that was a lie. However, she refused to allow her lingering fear to control her.

"All right, Mr. Franklin," she said levelly. "But you'll have to wait until I feed these three, or there'll be a rebellion. They're used to eating earlier than this. Why don't you wait in the living room?" Although phrased as a suggestion, her intonation made this last statement an order.

Deciding that, for the moment, retreat was the better part of valor, Bradley nodded and left. Reaching the living room, he realized he was still carrying his briefcase. After setting it down on the floor beside the highly polished, cherry-wood coffee table, he slowly wandered around the room. He noted that all of the breakable objects had been placed high up, out of reach of small hands, and recalled that he'd done the same thing to avoid always having to say "Don't touch" to his sister's children. The couch and chairs were a heavy, overstuffed style in muted blues and greens. They looked comfortable and inviting. A playpen in the corner held an assortment of toys. A newspaper had been thrown on the couch, unread. All in all, it was the kind of room he would have expected to find in a home filled with love and laughter. It was not what he'd expected to find in Annabelle Royd's home.

"Maybe she hired an interior decorator," he muttered under his breath. But when he recalled the woman who had answered the door, he could believe she created this room herself. Annabelle was an enigma. And he wasn't going to find out the truth about her or Swynite Industries by hanging around this room.

Reaching a decision, he removed his suit coat and tossed it onto the back of a chair. His tie followed. Then, rolling up his shirtsleeves, he walked back to the kitchen. "I've helped feed my niece and nephew," he said as he entered. "I'm not an expert but I'm pretty good. How about if I help?"

Annabelle had been so busy spooning food into three mouths, she hadn't heard him approaching. Startled by the sound of his voice, she glanced over her shoulder. The fit of his shirt gave definition to the broad strength of his shoulders. The hair-dusted arms revealed by the rolled-up sleeves were firm and sinewy. Without his suit coat on, she could see that his waist was trim and his abdomen flat. Here was a man who kept himself in top physical form. Again she experienced a curious curling sensation down deep inside of her, immediately followed by an intense rush of fear. The urge to scream at him to get out or she would call the police was nearly overwhelming. *Then he'd really think I was a hysterical fool,* she chided herself, her throat constricting from her effort to control this impulse. Levelly she said instead, "I'm doing just fine. Your help is really unnecessary."

Again Bradley was certain he'd seen a flash of terror in her eyes. During the preliminary research he'd done on this job before coming to Pittsburgh, he'd gone over the company's financial records thoroughly. He'd been certain the finances were in order. But the last time someone had acted this way toward him, he'd discovered massive embezzlement. Now was not the time to back off. "Looks like Jack could use a fellow male around to even the odds," he said, ignoring the unspoken command in her voice for him to leave. Rounding the table, he pulled up a seat beside the boy's high chair. "I assume this is his food," he added, taking possession of the divided plastic plate on the table in front of Jack.

"Yes," Annabelle replied. P. Bradley Franklin reminded her of a steamroller. Once he'd determined his direction, it seemed impossible to stop him.

"Okay, Jack, let's show these ladies how to eat," Bradley said.

The deeply ingrained fear Annabelle could not entirely shake was tempered by curiosity. In her wildest flight of imagination, she would never have envisioned P. Bradley Franklin spooning beef stew into an eleven-month-old child. And the truth was, he was doing a fairly good job of it. Even more surprising was that Jack was cooperating. He didn't usually accept strangers easily, and normally he was the messiest eater. When Bradley offered him the first spoonful, the boy had looked dubious; then it was as if an immediate male bonding had occurred, and Jack began eating neatly and rapidly.

Annabelle noted that the girls seemed stunned by Mr. Franklin's presence. Both had settled down and were allowing her to feed them with ease while they watched P. Bradley Franklin with fascination.

Well, he is the sort of man women consider interesting, she admitted, trying to concentrate on feeding her nieces but instead finding her attention constantly drawn to the man on the other side of the table. The fact that he honestly seemed to be enjoying himself shocked her. But what really shook her was how natural he looked in this setting. She had the sudden vision of him as a father sitting among his own children. And she was there as his wife. Then abruptly the vision was gone as a hard knot of fear coiled inside of her. *My mind is slipping,* she thought frantically. *P. Bradley Franklin might have a family one day, but it won't be with me.*

"Looks like we won, old fellow," Bradley said, spooning the last of the food into the boy's mouth.

Annabelle frowned. Her wild flights of imagination had made her nerves even more taut. "Do you treat everything like a contest, Mr. Franklin?" she heard herself asking. The question startled her. Then she told herself that it was legitimate. She hadn't been able to put her finger on it until just this moment, but now she realized that the way he was going through the company's records gave the impression that he considered himself in competition with the existing management.

"I suppose I do," he admitted. He rose, went over to the sink, wet a paper towel and returned to wipe the child's face and hands. His gaze narrowed on her. "That's why I'm so good at what I do. I face each job as a challenge I intend to win."

There was no perceivable threatening edge to his voice, yet Annabelle had the feeling she was being warned. Randall Swynite was probably very smart to keep his son away from P. Bradley Franklin, she decided.

"What now?"

Annabelle glanced toward Bradley, certain she'd heard impatience in his voice. She'd been right. She could see it in his eyes. Well, he was the one who'd insisted on helping, she thought. After their dinner, the babies had needed to be changed. She usually left two in the playpen and took the third upstairs to the large guest bathroom. It had a wide counter by the sink, and she'd change them one at a time. But Mr. Franklin had insisted on carrying the other two up. Now he stood in the doorway, holding the two she had already changed, watching her finish with Sarah.

"They play until their parents come to pick them up in a couple of hours," she replied. "If I put them to bed, they'll be up in the middle of the night." Even more important, she liked the security of not being alone with this man.

Bradley's stomach growled, reminding him he hadn't eaten. Finding a pair of very dark brown eyes suddenly looking at him questioningly, he said, "I didn't take the time to grab anything to eat before I came."

Annabelle was tempted to suggest that he go have a nice dinner, get a good night's rest and then they could go over his questions in the office the next morning. Instead she heard herself saying, "I was going to fix myself a sandwich. Would you like one?" Surprised that she'd made the offer, she quickly returned her attention to Sarah.

"Sure," Bradley replied, watching her in the mirror. Sarah had just smiled and rattled off some babbling babyish nonsensical sounds, causing Annabelle to grin at her and reply in soft teasing tones. Suddenly, for one brief second, he found himself picturing these children as his... picturing this as a typical evening at home with his family. His body tensed. Why he would be having such thoughts in the presence of Ms. Annabelle Royd completely baffled him. She most definitely wasn't the kind of woman he was looking for in a wife.

He did plan to marry and have a family one day. But he wanted an old-fashioned girl, one who would happily remain at home with the children, taking care of them, the house and him. Admittedly he sometimes wondered if such women still existed or if they were simply a myth created by the wishful male mind. Even his own mother had never waited on his father hand and foot. She'd had her volunteer work, and after he and his sister had all left home, she'd gone out and gotten a part-time job.

But Annabelle Royd! The one thing he was certain about her was that she loved her work. No, this was not a woman who would ever consider remaining home to raise a family. She was a dyed-in-the-wool career woman. In addition to that, he didn't trust her.

And right now, I'm beginning to worry about me, too, he added, still unable to believe he'd experienced that brief moment of insanity. But as he followed her down the stairs, he couldn't help noticing that she had a very pleasant swing to her hips. *What I need is a good night's sleep,* he decided as they reached the first floor. "I've changed my mind about that sandwich," he said, striding into the living room and placing the two babies he was carrying into the playpen. "With these three around, it's obvious to me we can't get any work done tonight. I'll just grab a bite at my hotel and then turn in. We can tackle my questions tomorrow."

He was picking up his coat, tie and briefcase and moving toward the door as he spoke.

Annabelle barely had time to say a quick goodbye before he was gone. As the front door closed behind him, she glanced at Sarah. "Well, he certainly got tired of our company in a big hurry," she said. She'd meant for this statement to come out with a touch of dry humor, but instead her voice carried a note of what sounded like regret. She frowned at herself. His quick exit had left her feeling confused. She told herself she was glad he was gone. Still, she suddenly felt strangely alone.

Chapter Three

Bradley was not in a good mood. He hadn't slept well. He'd dreamed of Annabelle Royd in jail, staring out at him from behind bars with those dark mahogany eyes of hers. The triplets had been there, too. She was holding the girls and Jack was hanging on to her leg, staring up at Bradley as if he was the devil himself. In the dream, Bradley was standing on the other side of the barred door with a huge ring of jailer's keys. He was telling Annabelle that crooks belonged in jail. In spite of the fact that he truly believed this, all the time he was speaking he was experiencing a hard knot of regret in his stomach.

He'd ordered himself to forget the dream, but the tenseness with which he had awakened remained. It had helped when Annabelle had come into the office dressed in a suit, her hair severely pulled back and wound into a tight coil, and her manner cold and standoffish. But he hadn't been able to entirely erase the image of her in jeans with her hair in disorder. Periodically he'd find himself glancing toward her and picturing a tendril escaping from the tight knot at the nape of her neck and hanging loosely over her cheek.

Annabelle was trying very hard to concentrate only on the paper in front of her and not the man beside her. But her concentration was hampered by tiredness. She hadn't slept well. Every time she'd closed her eyes, P. Bradley Franklin's image had filled her mind. When she'd fallen asleep, she'd dreamed of him. In the dream, he pulled her into his arms and kissed her. Halfway through the kiss, she awoke in a cold sweat. She'd ended up watching an hour of late-night television before she'd been able to get back to sleep.

This morning she awoke taut and strained. She hadn't wanted to face him. But the chill in his manner had eased her tension.

It was now noon, and Bradley's patience was strained. He frowned at himself. This wasn't like him. Normally he faced each job with calm detachment. Maintaining a distance between himself and the people he was investigating allowed him to present a fair and unbiased report based on facts and observation rather than emotionally influenced opinions. This was what made him one of the top business analysts in the country. But the thought of sending Annabelle to jail made him uncomfortable. It was seeing her with those babies that had done it. The woman seated beside him, who had spent the morning coolly feeding information to him like a human computer, did not need his sympathy nor deserve it. Still, he could not quite separate her from the woman with the gentle voice and loving touch. He wished he'd never gone to her home. He still wasn't certain why he had. *Something about a challenge,* he recalled.

They'd ordered lunch in. She'd taken a bite of her sandwich and now there was just a smidgen of mayonnaise at the corner of her mouth. Bradley had the strongest desire to lick it off with the tip of his tongue. *I don't even like mayonnaise,* he reminded himself.

Annabelle felt a prickling on the side of her neck. She knew it was because P. Bradley Franklin was looking at her. It bothered her that she was so aware of him. Normally the protective wall she kept around herself allowed her to ignore male inspections. But Mr. Franklin was a difficult man to ignore, and right now he was staring at her. Impatience hiding the uneasiness his gaze was causing, she glanced toward him.

"Mayonnaise," he said brusquely, and pointed to the corner of his mouth.

She flushed with embarrassment that quickly turned to anger. He'd said it as if he'd found some horrible defect in her. Well, she'd never claimed to be perfect. With dignity she picked up her napkin and wiped the offending blemish away.

Bradley chewed and swallowed a bite of his sandwich. It felt like a rock as it hit his stomach. He scowled at the food in front of him, then he turned to Annabelle. "There is something you should know."

Annabelle looked at him. His tone of voice had made this sound like a threat. If any man could intimidate her it was P. Bradley Franklin, but at the moment she was too tense to allow mere intimidation to bother her. "What should I know?" she asked with a calmness that belied the agitated state of her nerves.

"I've brought in an accountant I know and trust to do a thorough audit." He watched her as he made this statement. He saw confusion and surprise but no terror.

Annabelle shrugged. "We had a complete audit barely two months ago, and I was under the impression that you went over the books before you came." As the implication of what he'd just said sank in, her calm gaze turned to a glare. Edward Swynite might have a few ill-conceived ideas of what he wanted to do with the company, but none of them included anything dishonest. "However," she continued frostily, "you've been given full access by the board. You may do as you wish. I assume they're paying you by the job not the hour or the number of employees you bring in. Whatever way you choose to spend your resources is up to you."

That look of self-righteous indignation might cover a multitude of sins, he told himself. But his gut instinct told him that he'd been wrong to suspect embezzlement. Maybe she was just very nervous about her job. Some people completely froze when it came to being tested. Annabelle didn't strike him as that kind of person, but then he'd never expected to see a side of her that wore jeans and handled three small children with a motherly touch. "Tell me, Ms. Royd, how do you envision my report affecting you?" he asked bluntly.

The thought that this man could affect her life in any way at all irritated Annabelle. Having control over her own destiny was very important to her. But she was a practical woman. She knew that she would have to make compromises and that others would always be able to put some pressure on her or provide road-blocks. However, P. Bradley Franklin was definitely getting on her nerves, and she hated admitting that he could cause her any grief. She was tempted to tell him that he could write what he wished; it wouldn't bother her one way or the other. That, however, would be a lie and he'd know it.

"If your report is favorable toward the Swynites," she said, "and Edward is allowed to move into his father's position when Randall retires, then I'll move in here and become vice president of marketing. If your report is not favorable, then Edward will prob-ably remain where he is and I'll remain where I am."

"And Randall will throw a tantrum the size of Texas," Bradley added, amazed that she'd been so frank. But then he was constantly being amazed by her.

"And Randall will throw a tantrum the size of this continent," she corrected. Then, because she ad-mired the older Swynite, she added, "But he'll do it with dignity and in private."

Bradley could not fault her loyalty. In fact he liked it. And her concern over her career could be what was making her tense. A vice presidency was a big goal for a woman, especially one as young as she was. "It must be hard for him to have to answer to a board of direc-tors. If he'd realized he was going to lose control of his company, I wonder if he'd have ever offered shares to outside investors."

"He needed capital for new ventures," Annabelle said. She could still see the fury in Randall's eyes the day he discovered that not only was his daughter getting a divorce but that his former son-in-law was going to retain control of a percentage of her shares. It wasn't a large percentage, but it was just enough to rip the control of the company from his hands. "He'd always planned on maintaining a majority of the shares."

Bradley nodded. He knew about the bitter divorce and the battle between Howard Zyle, the company's second-largest shareholder, and Randall Swynite. He was also aware that Randall had offered his former son-in-law, a man by the name of Gerald Muldarn, triple the going rate for his shares. But Gerald Muldarn apparently had a vindictive bent. Instead of accepting Randall's offer, he'd sold his shares to Howard Zyle for less than what Randall had offered. And that sale had given Howard an even firmer grip on the company. It had been Howard who had forced the retirement-age clause into the company's bylaws, and it had been Howard who had coerced the rest of the board members into agreeing to have Bradley investigate the running of the company instead of merely handing the reins over to Edward Swynite.

"You've nothing to fear from me, Ms. Royd. I brought no bias with me. If Edward Swynite is doing a good job, and it appears that he is, my report will not cost him the presidency of this company."

Annabelle breathed an inward sigh of relief. She felt certain the company would do as well with Edward as president as it had with his father in that position.

Granted, Edward had some unorthodox ideas, but the board could control those. In the few instances when Randall had been forced to allow Edward to handle a business deal, Edward had displayed a business acumen as keen as his father's. In addition to that, Randall would still be chairman of the board. Since he could control his son, he would still, in all practicality, continue running the company as he always had. This, Annabelle knew, was precisely why Howard Zyle had instigated this investigation. He wanted Edward out and someone of his choosing—someone he could control—in. "I'm glad to hear that," she replied, then returned her attention to her lunch.

Seven o'clock came unexpectedly. Annabelle had been so deeply engrossed in going over files with Bradley she hadn't noticed when the rest of the staff left for the day.

"Looks like we're here alone," he said, shoving the last of the files aside, then stretching.

Annabelle glanced at the clock, only then realizing how late it was. She and Bradley were most likely the only two people on this floor. The nervousness that had faded while she'd concentrated on business matters returned.

"I think we've done enough for today," he was saying as he stretched a second time, then let his body relax. "How about some dinner?"

Bradley blinked. He couldn't believe he'd actually made that offer. He had no desire to spend time outside of the office with Annabelle.

Annabelle had been gazing toward the window trying not to think of the very virile male beside her. His invitation stunned her. She'd been certain he would be glad to be rid of her. A part of her wanted to make a polite refusal, then bolt out of the office and head for the security of her home. But another part, a bit of her down deep inside, wanted to accept the invitation. He'd only invited her to dinner, she pointed out to herself. That should be harmless enough.

"But then, I suppose you have better things to do with your time. You're probably sick and tired of my company, too," Bradley added quickly, wondering what insanity had prompted him to ask her to dine with him. Most likely, she'd spend the entire meal coolly tolerating him. Or maybe she'd suddenly become one of those women who couldn't stop talking, and he'd end up listening to her life story with a couple of her favorite dinner recipes thrown in. It suddenly occurred to him that he wouldn't mind hearing her life story, and that realization shook him.

Annabelle caught the impatient edge in his voice. He'd issued the invitation, but he hadn't meant it. *He probably thinks he owes me dinner because he kept me here so late,* she decided. She felt a fleeting sting of hurt. Then she assured herself that she was glad. It was now clear that she still needed to exorcise a few demons, but he certainly wasn't the one to help her. "You're right on both counts," she said, and rising from the table, began to arrange the files.

You asked for that one, Bradley told himself. He also told himself that he should feel relieved that she'd refused. *And I do,* he added firmly. This restlessness he was feeling had nothing to do with her. He thought of Brenda. He had her phone number in his pocket, but the thought of the other woman left him cold. "I'll walk you to your car," he said, telling himself that he'd make this offer to any woman he'd kept late in a large, nearly deserted building complex like this.

"That's really unnecessary," she assured him, still feeling the sting of insult caused by his less-than-enthusiastic dinner invitation.

"She's telling the truth. Ann has a black belt in karate," a male voice said from the doorway. "Now you know everything. She's not only my valued assistant but my bodyguard as well."

Annabelle turned to see Edward entering the office. He'd made this jest before in front of customers, and she'd accepted it with good humor. But this time it left a sour taste in her mouth. He made her feel like an Amazon with a mannish bearing and a total lack of femininity. But then, wasn't that how she presented herself to the world?

Bradley gave Annabelle another mark for surprise, then immediately mocked himself. Why should he be startled by the discovery of this accomplishment of hers? Actually, a skill in the martial arts seemed to suit her a great deal more than taking care of triplets. *She is definitely occupying too much of my mind,* he mused dryly. Ordering himself to concentrate on business, he focused his full attention on Edward Swynite. He was supposed to evaluate the man. To be totally accurate and fair, he should spend some time with him. "I was just on my way to dinner. How about joining me?"

For a moment, Edward hesitated. Then like a warrior rising to a challenge, he smiled. "Sure. I don't have any plans."

Annabelle knew that Randall would want her to go along to be certain Edward presented a conservative facade. But P. Bradley Franklin had made it clear he wasn't interested in having her around and she had her pride. Besides, Edward could handle himself. He knew how much was riding on his conduct. "If you gentlemen will excuse me," she said, already moving toward the door, "I'll be on my way."

She noted that they barely acknowledged her departure as Edward began suggesting places they could call for dinner reservations.

During the drive home, her agitation grew. But it wasn't directed at P. Bradley Franklin. It was directed at herself. Grudgingly she admitted that she found Mr. Franklin attractive, and it was that feeling of attraction that had her nerves on edge. "It would appear that I haven't been as successful in putting the past behind me as I thought," she murmured. But of all the men in the world, why did it have to be P. Bradley Franklin who wakened her to this fact?

Much later that night, Randall paced his study floor, his expression one of fury. "I suppose you talked to him about some of your ideas for the future of the company?" he demanded so loudly the words reverberated off the walls.

Edward sat in a chair beside the fireplace, glowering up at his father. He'd come by to tell him about his dinner with Bradley. As far as Edward was concerned it had been a success. Disgruntledly he told himself that he should have known Randall wouldn't see it that way, though. "Yes, we talked about the future," he replied, keeping his voice calm. One bellowing bull was enough, he decided. "The man's not archaic. He knows you can't run a business today the same way they did in medieval times."

Randall stopped his pacing to glare at his son. "I have tried to explain to you that the board *is* conservative. What they consider sensible, levelheaded business practices may seem archaic to you, but at the moment they're pulling the strings."

"Well, what's done is done," Edward replied. "And I honestly don't think Bradley's going to present me in an unacceptable light."

Randall's jaw firmed. "We can't take that chance. We must come up with a way to discredit Mr. Franklin should it be necessary."

Chapter Four

Annabelle shivered against the cold, moisture-laden wind as she hurried from the small country store to her car. It was nearly 9:00 p.m. It had been snowing lightly when she'd left Pittsburgh a couple of hours earlier. Here in the mountains the white flakes were much larger and falling faster.

She reached her car and put the bag of groceries on the front seat. Already the roads were getting treacherous. Accepting Randall's offer of his mountain cabin for the weekend had seemed like a good idea four hours ago. This week had been a strain.

Her reactions to P. Bradley Franklin had forced her to face a very unpleasant truth. Over the past eight years she'd assured herself a million times that what had happened that summer night in June hadn't left any permanent damage. She'd even dated some to

prove this was true. But none of the men she'd dated
had caused any stirrings of interest within her.

"I've been lying to myself all this time," she admitted for the tenth time that day as she slid in behind
the wheel and put the key into the ignition. "In spite
of all my reading and my determination to live a nor-
mal life, I'm afraid of having an intimate relationship."

She breathed a heavy sigh. She'd been so sure that
when a man came along to whom she was attracted,
she would be able to respond to that attraction. Instead, she was fleeing to the mountains like a frightened rabbit.

"Not fleeing," she corrected, as she guided the car
out of the parking lot. "I came up here to think. There
is nothing to flee *from*. I'm the last woman on earth
Mr. P. Bradley Franklin would take a second look at.
He didn't even take a first."

She'd been smiling at this bit of self-mockery. Suddenly her car threatened to skid and the smile vanished. "It might have been a better idea to do my soul-
searching at home," she muttered. The road conditions were getting worse. The snow that had fallen
before dark had melted. When darkness had come and
the temperature had dropped, that melted snow had
frozen into a thin layer of ice. Now there was a full two
inches of the white stuff on top of the ice and the
depth of this new snow was increasing rapidly. She
frowned at the road ahead. There was only another ten
miles to go, she told herself encouragingly. She could
make it.

"And I have," she said with relief a while later as she turned off the main road. The falling snow was now so dense, she'd almost missed the three-quarter-mile private drive that led to the cabin.

Actually "cabin" did not adequately describe the residence, she mused, as she guided the car up the long, narrow roadway. Randall always referred to this place as his "little log cabin in the woods," giving the impression that it was small and rustic. True, it *was* made of logs, but the "cabin" was equipped with all the conveniences that could be found in any modern home. It even had an electric generator so that if the power lines were knocked out by the weather, the cabin still had electricity.

And Annabelle would never have considered it small. The two-story structure had nearly double the space she had in her entire house. A wide porch encircled the dwelling, giving a welcoming air. Inside, the first floor had an open design. With the exception of a portion enclosed to create a spacious bathroom, the rest of the area was one huge room. A fully equipped kitchen occupied the wall opposite the front entrance. A fireplace big enough for a child to stand in dominated the south wall. Bookshelves, a gun rack and a well-stocked bar were along the north wall. A long, rough-hewn table with benches along both sides and captain's chairs at either end provided a place to eat in the kitchen-dining portion of the space. Invitingly, overstuffed leather furniture was arranged throughout the living-room area with a very cozy grouping near the fireplace. Eight massive support pillars, each the width of a good-sized tree trunk, were the only interruptions to the openness. Upstairs was a master bedroom suite with a private bath, three guest rooms and another bathroom.

Annabelle had been here a couple of times before at Randall's request. Edward refused to come because he didn't like the isolation. The nearest civilization was the small country store where she'd purchased her supplies. So, at times when work had been done on the cabin and Randall hadn't been able to get away from Pittsburgh to make a personal inspection, he'd asked her to go and see that everything was in order. She'd been happy to do this because she loved the mountains, and the isolation suited her.

Annabelle squinted in an attempt to see better as she reached the wide parking area in front of the cabin and came to a stop. A puzzled expression descended over her features. The lights in the cabin were on, and there was a car parked near the steps leading up to the porch. The vehicle was already thickly covered with snow, making it impossible for her to identify the make or model. It occurred to her that it might belong to Ida Crowe. Ida, Annabelle knew, lived about fifteen miles away, near Rossiter, Pennsylvania. Randall had employed her for years. Once every two weeks she drove up here to clean the place so that it was always ready for occupancy. But she usually did her work during the week.

I suppose she might have been busy and couldn't get here until today and now the snow's trapped her, Annabelle reasoned. *Or the car might belong to a stranger who's using the cabin uninvited,* she thought anxiously. Contemplating turning around and leaving, she glanced into her rearview mirror. All she could see was white. In just the minute she'd been stopped, the back window had been completely covered with snow.

She turned her attention back to the cabin. Suddenly the front door opened and the occupant was illuminated by the porch light. Annabelle blinked in disbelief. It wasn't Ida or a stranger. It was P. Bradley Franklin.

"What the devil is he doing here?" she muttered, as a flood of reactions swept over her. The first was panic. This was quickly followed by a very feminine recognition of how ruggedly handsome he looked in this setting. "I came up here to ease my frayed nerves, and now they feel as if they're ready to become completely unraveled," she groaned.

Her back stiffened. He was coming toward her car. "Get a grip on yourself," she ordered as she opened the door and stepped out.

For a second Bradley wondered if he was hallucinating. The last person he'd expected to see up here was Annabelle. "What are you doing here?" he asked as he reached her.

"Randall offered me the cabin for the weekend," she replied, still unable to believe this was happening. She'd braved this storm to put distance between herself and this man and here he was standing right in front of her!

Bradley frowned impatiently. "I don't understand. Edward arranged for me to come up here. He and his father were supposed to join me tomorrow for a relaxing weekend." He scowled skyward. "This snowfall was supposed to be light. It wasn't supposed to be more than a couple of inches.''

Annabelle's uneasiness was building. "I was under the impression that you never relax," she said, blurting out the first thing that came to mind. It was a stupid remark, she chided herself, but she'd felt the need to say something.

Bradley studied her. The very cool Ms. Royd was clearly rattled. Well, he wasn't too pleased with this turn of events, either. "I don't usually when I'm on a job. Truth is, I wanted to observe the two of them together outside of the office before I wrote up my final evaluations."

Annabelle glanced over her shoulder, hoping to see another set of car lights. There were none. "Well, someone got his signals crossed." She, too, frowned up at the sky. "And it's my guess that no one is going to be able to drive up here tomorrow. This is definitely more than a two-inch fall, and it's still coming down."

"And no one's going to be driving out of here tonight, either," Bradley added, looking beyond her to the long driveway. Already the tracks she'd made only minutes before were almost obliterated. "There's got to be four or five inches of snow on the roads by now. It's a wonder you got here without having an accident or getting stuck."

His voice held a reprimand that suggested he thought that, by driving up here, she had behaved foolishly. She stiffened in defiance. "It wasn't snowing this hard when I left Pittsburgh. And, as you pointed out, this wasn't supposed to be a heavy snow.

By the time the conditions got worse and I heard a revised forecast predicting four to six inches, I was closer to here than home." She didn't add that at the time she hadn't minded the thought of getting snowed in up here. She'd been in search of solitude.

Bradley drew a terse breath. Annabelle Royd. Of all the women he knew, she would have been his last choice of someone to be stranded with. However, he was stuck, and he might as well accept it. "We'd better go inside before we freeze," he said. "I'll get your luggage." He held his hand out for her keys.

"I can get my own luggage," she replied as she frantically calculated the odds of getting safely to the nearest motel. At the moment they weren't good. Even if she could get down the drive, he was right about the amount of the snow piling up on the main road. It would be treacherous and she hadn't seen any road crews out working to clear it yet. *I can handle this,* she assured herself. *He'll probably ignore me the entire time we're here.* Bowing to the inevitable, she opened the trunk of her car.

Little Miss Independence, Bradley mused. He was tempted to leave her on her own, but it was cold, wet and slippery. *And if she gets sick or injured, I'll have to take care of her,* he told himself, searching for a reason to explain the sudden strong concern he felt. "No sense in your having to make two trips." Reaching around her, he picked up the suitcase. "I'll take this. You grab your groceries."

As she followed him inside, Annabelle noticed that the cabin seemed about half its usual size. "I can't believe the Swynites made such a mistake," she murmured.

Bradley was having a hard time believing it himself. Now if Brenda had shown up, he'd have known it was no mistake. But Annabelle? "I took the guest room at the far corner facing west," he said, already starting up the stairs. "I'll put you in the one on the east corner."

If he'd simply come out and said he preferred to keep as much distance between them as possible, he couldn't have been clearer, Annabelle thought as she nodded to his disappearing back. Well, that suited her just fine. Carrying the bag of groceries to the table in the kitchen area, she set it down and began unpacking it.

"Looks like we won't starve," Bradley said as he joined her. He was attempting to find a bright side, but it wasn't easy. Not only did it look as if he wasn't going to have a chance to observe father and son together, he was trapped with the career women of the year. He frowned at himself. Normally he never let a female's choice of life-style bother him. If Annabelle's goal in life was to run a company, then he wished her well, he assured himself. Directing his mind back to food, he added, "The freezer is stocked, and I stopped and picked up a few things myself."

Annabelle turned toward him. It took a concerted effort to keep from staring. He'd removed his coat and now she saw that he was dressed in old jeans and a sweater. His snow-wet hair was mussed and a lock had fallen onto his forehead. She didn't think she'd ever seen a man look more appealing. A hard knot suddenly formed in her abdomen while a cold sweat broke out on the palms of her hands. Quickly she swung her gaze to the remaining groceries. "I can't believe this mix-up," she said.

"I find it a little hard to believe myself," Bradley replied. But he hadn't been able to come up with any logical explanation for why the father and son would play a trick like this.

Annabelle noted that the impatience in his voice had increased. Obviously being stuck here with her was not his idea of a fun way to spend the weekend. Well, it wasn't her idea of relaxing, either.

The ringing of the phone interrupted the uncomfortable silence that had fallen between them.

Bradley answered it.

It was Edward. "I just found out that my father offered the cabin to Ann for the weekend," he said. "It never occurred to me he would do that. Did she get there all right? The weather got rotten pretty fast."

"She's here," Bradley replied grimly, then added, "Next time, I'd suggest you check with your father before you make plans." He was tempted to ask how the father and son planned to run a business together if they couldn't get their arrangements for a simple weekend straight. But telling himself that venting his anger wouldn't help, he held his tongue. Stoically he listened to a profuse apology, then forced himself to say evenly, "Mistakes happen."

Edward then asked to speak to Annabelle.

"I'm so sorry about this," he said the moment Annabelle came on the line. "It never occurred to me that my father would offer the place to you."

Annabelle frowned into the receiver. "I'm finding it hard to believe that you would arrange to meet anyone up here," she said, still having trouble accepting this situation. "You hate coming up here."

"I did some checking. When he's not working, Bradley has a place in the Rockies where he retreats to and plays hermit. I thought he'd feel at home at the cabin. And I had no idea this snow was going to be so heavy. I figured we'd get a light dusting," Edward explained apologetically.

She had to admit his reasoning was sound. She just wished she hadn't gotten caught in the middle of one of his schemes to win P. Bradley Franklin over to his side. "Next time I'll check with you before accepting any invitations from your father," she returned dryly.

"Don't worry. Call Ida," Edward instructed, and quickly gave Annabelle the number. "Her husband has a snowplow attachment for his Jeep. He'll come clear the drive, and the road crew will take care of the main road. Besides, the weather's supposed to warm up considerably tomorrow. By Sunday you should be able to get back to Pittsburgh without any trouble."

The words "by Sunday" echoed in her head as she hung up. *With any luck, we can be out of here tomorrow,* she told herself encouragingly.

In the meantime, she and Mr. Franklin could ignore one another for the major portion of the time they were closeted here. Considering his reactions to her, she was sure that would be a totally acceptable arrangement to him.

* * *

Edward turned toward his father as he replaced the receiver in the cradle. "They're both there and snowed in."

Randall was grinning broadly. "Bless these unexpected storms. Instead of spending only a short while together at the cabin, they'll be spending a full night. This is even better than I'd hoped. I can forget about my contingency plan."

"I still don't understand why you wanted the two of them up there together," Edward said, studying his father as if he thought Randall had come unglued. "They don't even like each other."

"Only you and I know that." A gleam came into Randall's eyes. "Just go along with me. Believe me, we can use this to our advantage."

While Randall was congratulating himself, Annabelle was phoning Ida and making arrangements for the woman's husband to come as quickly as he could and plow the drive.

"Sounds as if you've arranged for our rescue," Bradley said as she hung up. He'd heard her side of the conversation and knew she'd tried to get the man to come as soon as possible. He also guessed from her glum look that Mr. Crowe was not sure the road crews would have the main road cleared in time for him to do the job tomorrow. Mentally he cursed. He didn't like admitting it, but Annabelle made him uncomfortable. Looking out the window, he said hopefully, "I think the snow is coming down slower now."

Annabelle wandered over to a window in a different wall. "I think you're right," she replied, determined to be optimistic about an early escape.

For a long moment another heavy silence fell over the room. Then Bradley turned and strode toward the kitchen area. "As long as we're stuck here, we might as well make the best of it," he said in a resigned tone. "I'm pretty good at broiling steaks. How are you at salads?"

"Good enough," she replied, and moved toward the kitchen, also.

He noticed that she still had on her heavy parka. "I've got a fire going. It's fairly warm in here. You probably ought to take your coat off."

She grimaced as she admitted that, up until this very moment, she'd been hoping to find a way out of there. But there was no way out. Finally acknowledging that she was stuck at the cabin until help arrived, she removed her coat and hung it on a peg near the door. She'd changed into jeans and a sweater for the drive. Now she wished she was still in her business suit. She doubted that Mr. P. Bradley Franklin would even notice what she was wearing, but the staid tailored attire was like added physical insulation against the world.

Bradley caught a glimpse of her out of the corner of his eye. Damn, she looked cute in that outfit, he thought. But he still didn't want to be here with her. It was her uneasiness around him that bothered him, he decided. And there was no reason for her to be uneasy. She was very good at her job—excellent, in fact. Her career would not be damaged in any way by his report. Even if Edward wasn't given the presidency,

Annabelle would eventually reach her goal. Of that Bradley was certain.

What he still wasn't so certain about was whether this foul-up in weekend arrangements was a legitimate mistake or whether the Swynites had something up their sleeves. However, if they did have a reason for this little charade, he was pretty sure Annabelle wasn't in on it. He had the feeling that she would rather have been dragged over hot coals than be sequestered here with him. But whatever was going on, innocent or not so innocent, he couldn't do anything about it at the moment.

To Annabelle's relief, the next half hour passed reasonably quickly and smoothly as they both concentrated on preparing the meal. But when they sat down to eat, a heavy silence again descended between them, and she felt as though the walls were closing in on her. "I'm really sorry about this mix-up," she said. Then, because her nervousness was making it difficult for her to think clearly, she heard herself adding the thought that next popped into her mind. "I guess the only lucky thing about it is that you don't have a wife we would have to explain this to."

"And you don't have a husband or boyfriend," he added, willing to grab at any straw of conversation to lighten the tension.

She nodded and forced herself to take another bite of her steak. But swallowing wasn't easy. Butterflies seemed to be fluttering around in her stomach. Relax! she ordered herself.

Bradley covertly studied Annabelle. She intrigued him. But not in a personal way, he stipulated. It was simply that she was so contradictory. At work, she reminded him of a human computer. She was sternly businesslike. During the past few days at the offices of Swynite Industries, he'd never heard her laugh and seen her smile only twice. Then there was the Annabelle Royd he'd witnessed the night he'd gone to her home. She'd still been stilted in her behavior toward him, but with the children she'd shown a gentle side he'd never have believed she had if he hadn't seen it with his own eyes. Curiosity, he warned himself, could be a dangerous thing. Still, he heard himself asking, "Are you one of those women who devote all her energies to your career, or are you simply between men at the moment?"

Annabelle tensed. Once before she'd been too trusting. Had she misjudged P. Bradley Franklin? She met his gaze. There was nothing there or in his voice to make her think he was expressing a personal interest. She shrugged. "Between my career and babysitting my nieces and nephew every once in a while, I haven't had much time for a man in my life."

Mentally Bradley patted himself on the back. He'd been right. Ms. Royd was a dedicated career woman, basically cold at the core, at least where men were concerned.

Annabelle tried to concentrate on her meal, but she couldn't stop herself from thinking that turnabout was fair play. "And are you simply a single-minded, career-oriented person, or are you between women at the moment?" As soon as the question was out, she wished she hadn't asked. His personal life was of no concern to her.

"I travel a great deal. Because of that, I don't like to feel tied down to a particular relationship," he replied. The truth was, he simply hadn't found anyone who could hold his interest. Grudgingly he admitted that Annabelle interested him, but it wasn't personal, he assured himself. It was more of an intellectual exercise—an observation of the modern-day career woman.

She'd been right about Mr. Franklin, Annabelle congratulated herself. He was most definitely not the kind of man for her. A permanent relationship was the only type she would ever consider. This knowledge should also help to rid her of this unwanted attraction she felt toward him, she reasoned.

Bradley smiled crookedly. "My mother and sister keep telling me that I just haven't met the right woman." Returning his attention to his food, he wondered why he'd admitted that. Just making conversation, he told himself, then forced his full attention to his steak.

Annabelle's heart lurched at the sight of that smile. Unwillingly she found herself wondering what it would be like to be the *right* woman for P. Bradley Franklin. She suddenly broke out into a cold sweat. *Ignore him,* she ordered, forcing herself to concentrate on her meal.

Finally they were finished. Bradley glanced at his portable computer. Thank goodness he'd brought it along, he thought. The prospect of spending the evening trying to make stilted conversation with Annabelle, or the both of them simply staring at each other in silence, had his nerves growing more on edge by the moment.

Annabelle noticed the path of his gaze. It should be a relief that he's got work to keep himself occupied, she told herself. Still, she couldn't stop feeling a bit miffed. He made her feel less interesting than a chair. Mentally she laughed at herself. No doubt that was exactly how he viewed her. *And I should be happy about that,* she told herself. After all, he was not what she was looking for. Aloud she said, "If you want to get back to your work, I'll do the dishes. Then I think I'll go on up to bed. It's been a long day."

Having her disappear upstairs, leaving him on his own, suited Bradley just fine. "Are you sure you don't want some help with the dishes?" he asked, determined to be a gentleman about this.

"I'm sure," she replied. The farther away from him she was, the better she liked it.

Nodding, Bradley left the table. Within minutes he was busy typing.

It took Annabelle very little time to clear up their dishes, then she went upstairs. She changed into a pair of heavy flannel pajamas and climbed into bed. Bradley, she'd noted, was so completely absorbed in his work, he hadn't even seen her leaving. She recalled the masculine approval in his eyes a few times when his gaze had fallen on Brenda during the past few days.

"I'll bet if she was here, he wouldn't be so single-minded about his work," she muttered. For one brief moment, she wondered how he would react if she tried to flirt with him, then the cold sweat returned. Frustration swept over her. "He's not the right man for me, anyway," she told herself again. Irritated that she was still allowing him to taunt her, she ordered herself to go to sleep. Being both physically and mentally exhausted, she obeyed.

Chapter Five

Bradley sat staring into the dying embers of the fire. It would be nice to have a warm, gentle woman sharing this moment with him, he thought. He cast a glance toward the stairs. Instead he was stuck here with the ice queen. It's just as well, he told himself philosophically. He didn't need any complications on this job. This report was shaping into a touchy business.

Leaning back, he closed his eyes. He knew he ought to go up and get some sleep. It had been a long day. Then he heard it. At first he thought maybe it was the wind. No, not the wind, he corrected. That last sound was definitely a human sob. Then came an anguished cry.

In the next instant, Bradley was on his feet, hurrying upstairs. The cries were coming from Annabelle's room.

"No! Stop! Don't!" he heard her pleading in a voice filled with fear and anger.

"What the devil?" he growled, wondering what or who could have gotten into her room. He glanced along the hall for a weapon. An antique cavalry sword hung on the wall, along with a bugle. He grabbed the sword, then tried to open her door. It was locked. With a firm kick directly above the knob, he sent it flying open. The room was dark. In the light shining in from the hall all he could discern was Annabelle, in her bed, struggling violently.

Hoping the light switch was in the same position in this room as it was in his own, he found it and flipped it on. The lamp on the table to the right of the door came on.

He moved toward the bed, the sword in striking position. Annabelle had kicked off her covers, giving him a full view of whatever she was struggling against. But there was nothing attacking her. "She must be having one hell of a nightmare," he murmured, noting that neither the light nor his noisy entrance had awakened her. As she continued fighting off her invisible foe, he paused to set the sword aside, then approached the bed.

Totally trapped in her dream, Annabelle was fighting as she had never fought before, but as usual, she was losing. A loud crash in the background almost distracted the big male pinning her down long enough for her to escape, but then she was at his mercy once again. She heard a voice crying out and realized it was her own. Like every time before no rescuer came.

"No, please, no!" she pleaded, tears spilling out of the corners of her eyes.

A fear for her gripped Bradley. He'd never seen anyone in such anguish. "Ms. Royd, wake up," he ordered. Reaching down, he shook her by the shoulders.

Annabelle's body tensed. A fresh flow of adrenaline pumped through her. She was determined that this time she would escape. In one swift movement she twisted away from the grasp on her shoulders and turned her body slightly so that she could aim her attack at the position from where the voice had come. In the next instant, her leg shot out in a side kick.

Bradley took the impact in the stomach. It knocked the breath out of him and sent him staggering backward into the dresser. "Damn!" he gasped as he fell against the brass knobs on the drawers.

Jarring pain from the blow traveled up Annabelle's leg. The dream faded slightly and reality began to intrude. The sound of a crash followed by cursing brought her to full wakefulness. She jerked around into a sitting position. The form of a man registered on her mind. In the next instant she was on her feet in a karate attack posture.

"Hold it right there, lady!" Bradley ordered, extending one hand out in front of him the way a traffic cop would to stop a car. The fear he'd felt for her was gone. In its place was the worry that *he* might need some protection.

Annabelle halted in midmotion, then drew back into a defensive posture as panic gave way to rational thought and she remembered where she was and who he was. As she grew even more alert, she saw that Bradley was standing slightly bent, holding his abdomen with the arm that wasn't extended toward her. Obviously the kick she'd performed in her dream had not been merely in her mind. "What are you doing in my bedroom?" she demanded.

"You were crying out for help," he replied, through teeth clenched in pain. Continuing to hold his abdomen, he straightened away from the dresser. "I thought you needed rescuing. Obviously I was mistaken. You could take on an army single-handedly." Still keeping his arm extended toward her to ward off any further attack, he moved toward the door. Pausing for a moment in the doorway, he glanced at the splintered wood. "Don't know why you bothered to lock it," he muttered. Then, with a shake of his head, he continued on down the hall.

A flush of embarrassment had spread from the top of Annabelle's head to the tip of her toes as she sank down onto the bed and stared at the open door. She felt terrible about having hurt him. Suddenly the thought that she might have injured him seriously brought her back to her feet. She grabbed her robe from the nearby chair, pulled it on and hurried after him.

She heard the door of his room closing as she left her room. It occurred to her that she was probably the last person in the world he wanted to see at the moment. But she didn't stop. She had to make certain he was all right.

Outside his room, she hesitated for a moment, sure her reception would not be pleasant. Then she knocked.

When he opened the door, the sight of him caused her to step back a pace. He was bare from the waist up. Curls of thick, blondish brown hair formed a V in the center of the firmly defined musculature of his chest and abdomen. His shoulders were broad and strong. There wasn't an ounce of flab visible. A womanly appreciation of his physique caused a warm curling within her, then she again broke out in a cold sweat. "I'm sorry," she apologized shakily.

"Maybe you should consider wearing a sign that reads Approach with Caution," he suggested.

Annabelle had the sudden urge to cry. He made her feel frustrated and foolish and like a damnable menace. "I said I was sorry," she returned stiffly, then turning abruptly, she strode back down the hall. A headache had begun to build. When she reached the stairs she went down them to the kitchen in search of aspirin. There was a bottle in the cupboard and she took two. Too restless and upset to return immediately to her room, she wandered over to the fireplace and stood staring down at the dying embers. Hot tears burned at the back of her eyes. She wanted desperately to put the past behind her.

"Now, it's my turn to apologize."

She jerked around to see that Bradley had joined her. He was standing about eight feet away as if he wasn't certain it was safe to get any closer. "How do you feel?" she asked. "Do you think I did any real damage?" Anxiety spread through her. What would they do if he needed a doctor? They were snowed in, and she doubted that any one could get to them easily.

"Nothing permanent," he assured her. She looked so distraught he was furious with himself for having made that crack upstairs and upsetting her even more. An urge to wrap his arms around her protectively came over him. But remembering how dangerous she could be, he prudently chose to keep his distance. "Maybe a cracked rib," he said teasingly, attempting to lighten her mood, then added with a crooked smile, "but it only hurts when I laugh."

Annabelle chewed on her bottom lip. He was joking, trying to make her feel better. But she continued to regard him worriedly. "Seriously, are you sure we shouldn't call a doctor? Maybe there's one nearby with a snowmobile who would come here and check you over."

"I'll be all right," he said firmly. The smile faded as he continued to study her. Being curious about Annabelle Royd had proved disconcerting in the past, he reminded himself. But instead of heeding this warning, he heard himself saying, "That was some nightmare you were having. Do you have them often?"

This is none of your business, he told himself curtly as soon as the question was asked. Still, he was more interested in the answer than he wanted to admit.

Unable to face him, she turned her attention back toward the fire. "It's been a while since I had one. I was hoping they'd stopped."

Bradley watched her. There was a sense of fragility about her. *There is nothing fragile about that woman,* he chided himself. He had the bruises to prove it. *Say good-night, wish her better dreams and go to bed,* he ordered himself. Instead, he heard himself asking, "Is it a recurring nightmare or a different one each time?"

Annabelle's jaw trembled. "The same." The face of a man in his twenties filled her mind. It was a handsome face, with a deceptive boyish innocence.

Bradley would never have believed that Annabelle could look so vulnerable. *The woman just cracked a couple of your ribs,* he reminded himself. *These nightmares of hers are none of your business. Remember what curiosity did to the cat.* But again he didn't heed his own warning. Instead, he said, "You were struggling as if the devil himself had a hold on you."

Annabelle stared grimly into the red coals. "That's a good description of what it feels like." Suddenly, wide awake, she saw it happening to her again. Her hands balled into fists and hot tears burned behind her eyes. "I was raped."

She drew a startled breath. She couldn't believe she'd told P. Bradley Franklin. She hadn't even told her family. She'd reasoned that it would only upset them and there was nothing they could do about it, anyway. In a moment of honesty, she'd also admitted to herself that she just didn't want her parents to know. She knew they loved her, but she couldn't stop being afraid they might think that somehow she was just a little to blame for what had happened. She hadn't felt strong enough to face even a shadow of disappointment in their eyes. As for her sister, she knew Linda would have stood by her unflinchingly. But Linda was not good at keeping secrets. Even more, Linda was her kid sister. There was only a three-year difference in their ages, but Annabelle thought of Linda as being a naive, sweet, innocent soul, and she felt too protective toward her to share such an ugly truth. So, because of those reasons and others that involved her reputation, for the past eight years it had been Annabelle's secret. She'd planned on keeping it that way.

Rage toward the man who would do such a thing to a woman filled Bradley. Along with it came a surge of sympathy for Annabelle "Have you had counseling?"

A deeply rooted anger was beginning to come back to life within her. It was as if she had held all of this in too long, and now it was demanding to come out. "Some," she replied, talking more to herself than to him as the memories flooded back. "About four hours the night it happened."

Bradley studied the grim line of her jaw. He sensed her pain and it tore at him. "That's not much."

The hurt and humiliation she'd felt that night again swept over her. A bitterness mingled with her anger. "I couldn't return to the counseling center and I couldn't afford my own shrink."

Bradley frowned in confusion. "Why couldn't you return to the counseling center?"

The injustice of it all surged through her. "Because if I had, I would have ended up being the one with the police record."

Bradley's gaze narrowed. "That doesn't make any sense."

Annabelle couldn't believe she'd told him this much. All she'd meant to do was to apologize for hurting him. Now it occurred to her that he might consider looking into her past. She wasn't certain what repercussions that might cause. She'd suffered enough from the incident, and didn't want to take a chance on suffering more. She was going to have to tell him the rest and hope he would respect her privacy.

"It was a date rape," she said tersely. "And the man who did it was from a wealthy, influential family. He was captain of the college football team, president of his fraternity and an honor student." Unable to stand still, she began to pace around the room. "I was flattered when he asked me out. I wasn't in a sorority or involved in any of the major social functions on campus. The people he normally associated with wouldn't even give me the time of day. Where his crowd was concerned, I was a nobody. Actually, where anyone was concerned, I was a wallflower, to say the least. I spent most of my time studying or working. My parents couldn't afford to pay all my expenses, so I always had a part-time job. I didn't want to have to go into debt. And I had to study hard for my grades. I wasn't one of those people who could read something once and remember it perfectly."

Bradley found it hard to visualize Annabelle as a nobody. He'd thought of her as cold and impersonal, but she had a presence that made itself felt.

"Anyway, he took me to a party at his fraternity house. He was the perfect gentleman. His friends even kidded him about his behavior being more polite than usual." A bitter smile curled her lips. "I felt flattered that he was being extra nice because of me."

She stopped her pacing and stared out the window with unseeing eyes, her mind filled with images from the past. "I had an exam the next day so we left the party a little early. But he didn't take me directly back to the dorm like he'd said he would. Instead, he said he felt like going for a drive. I was having a really nice time so I didn't object. He drove out to a secluded place where there was a lake. Then he suggested we go sit on a blanket down by the water and talk. I didn't see any harm in that. But after we were sitting on the blanket he became more aggressive. I told him I wanted to go back to the dorm, but when I got up, he pulled me back down." Annabelle's stomach began to knot and the bile rose in her throat.

She started pacing again. "I tried to fight him off but he was stronger. Afterward, I remember him laughing. He'd dated me on a bet, he said. He'd lost a wager on a football game. A couple of the guys in his fraternity were in a few of my classes, and they chose me as his penalty. I'd been a virgin and that seemed to please him even more. Then he just drove off and left me there." Nausea swept over her.

"Are you all right?" Bradley asked, the paleness of her complexion worrying him. He was furious with himself for having allowed his curiosity to cause her to go through this. "Maybe you should sit down." He started toward her but stopped when she backed away.

Annabelle felt unclean, just the way she had that night. She wrapped her arms tightly around herself, fighting to hold back the nausea. Then her anger returned to overshadow all the other emotions tearing at her. "It took me two hours to walk back to campus. When I got there I went to the campus police and told them what had happened. They took me to the local hospital where the doctors made an examination, took samples and then provided a woman counselor I could talk to. In the meantime the police had gone to talk to Vance."

Annabelle still found what had happened next hard to accept. Frustration mingled with fury in her eyes. She came to an abrupt halt. With her hands clutching the back of a chair, she met Bradley's gaze. "The police came to see me the next morning. They said they'd talked to Vance and several of his friends. According to them, I'd been trying to seduce Vance all evening. Vance swore that I was the one who suggested the drive and I was the one who had come on to him. He said that I'd demanded money afterward and when he wouldn't give it to me I'd gotten violent. That was why he'd left me there and driven home alone. He told the police that this was just my way of getting revenge."

"And they believed him?" Bradley asked, already guessing the answer.

"Like I said, his family was very influential. It was my word against his and his friends. I'm not sure they believed him, but they had no choice." Annabelle dropped her gaze to her hands. "And I had no choice. He called me and let me know that if I persisted in my charges, if I even went back to the clinic for counseling, if I did anything other than let the matter vanish,

he would have his friends swear that I'd tried to so-
licit them and have me arrested for prostitution.''

She forced her hands to release their hold on the
chair. Her back straightened and she faced Bradley
with pride. "So it was up to me to work through it on
my own. I finished the semester and transferred to a
school in another state. In the meantime, I did a lot of
reading about rape and how to cope with it. In the
end, I concluded that it was up to me to put the incident behind me—not forget it, that would be impossible, but not to let it interfere with my life. And I
thought I had.''

"I suppose it was being sequestered here with me
that sparked the nightmare," Bradley said, wanting to
help her but not knowing how. The strength of his
desire to get his hands on this Vance character and beat
him to within an inch of his worthless life was close to
overwhelming.

"I suppose," she replied. She'd admitted enough
for a lifetime. She wasn't going to tell him that she felt
an attraction to him and that was what had brought
the nightmare back.

Annabelle Royd had proven to be a whole bag of
surprises, Bradley thought. "You don't have to be
afraid of me," he said gruffly. "I won't do anything
to harm you.''

Annabelle had to fight back the urge to laugh. His
lack of interest in her was obvious. "I know," she replied.

Bradley had never thought of himself as a vengeful
man, but he couldn't get the thought of this Vance
person out of his mind. The desire to see the man

punished was strong. For her sake, he told himself to drop the subject. But he couldn't. "Whatever happened to this Vance character?" he asked.

A wry look crossed Annabelle's face. "He died about six weeks later. He was driving drunk and crashed into a tree. Killed himself and his three passengers." An acid quality entered her voice. "His mother came to see me the day after the funeral. I remember her black dress was a designer original and she was wearing a little pillbox hat with a black veil that came down over her face. Her perfume was one of those six-hundred-dollars-an-ounce kind, and she was wearing some of the biggest diamonds I'd ever seen. She explained that Vance was her only child. Then she asked me if there was any chance I might be pregnant. If I was, she wanted me to have the baby and she'd pay me a hundred thousand dollars for it." An expression of distaste came over Annabelle's features. "I wouldn't have sold that woman a goldfish." Then she shrugged. "That, however, was academic. I wasn't pregnant. So she left me with a threat. She said if I ever told my story about her son to anyone, she'd ruin me." Her gaze narrowed on Bradley. "And I believe she'd do it. So I'd appreciate it if you'd just forget everything I've told you."

"I won't repeat it," he promised, but he knew he would never forget it. It explained a lot about Annabelle.

She suddenly felt exhausted. As she glanced up the stairs toward her room, she remembered the broken doorjamb.

"I'll have Ida's husband take care of repairing your door," Bradley said, his mind following the same path. "We'll tell the Swynites you were frightened by a mouse and refused to get off the chair to unlock the door, so I had to break it down to rescue you." The thought of her perched on a chair and him coming to her rescue pleased him, and he smiled.

Annabelle glanced at him and saw the crooked grin. There was a look of camaraderie in his eyes. They weren't friends and never would be, she knew, but he was on her side in this. "Thanks," she said gratefully, then went up to bed.

The next morning Annabelle was nervous about facing Bradley. She was still having a difficult time believing she'd told him about the rape.

"It's stopped snowing," he said as he came downstairs.

She was in the kitchen area making coffee. *Face him like nothing happened,* she ordered herself. "I know," she replied. "And I called Ida. She said the road crews were out last night and the main roads are passable. Her husband should be here anytime now. We'll be able to leave by midmorning."

Bradley nodded. He noticed that Annabelle had pulled her hair back into the severe style she wore at the office, and there were lines of strain on her face as if she hadn't slept well. But instead of finding her haggard appearance unappealing he was finding it sort of endearing. *I'm just feeling sympathy toward her because of her past,* he reasoned. "I make a pretty good omelet," he offered, opening the refrigerator door and peering inside.

Annabelle watched him turn away and wondered if he found it embarrassing to look at her now that he knew about the rape. He hadn't been interested in looking at her before, she reminded herself. "An omelet sounds good," she replied, determined not to care what he thought of her.

But when they sat down a little later to eat and a silence again descended between them, her nerves neared the breaking point. Frantically she searched for a topic that would take her thoughts off her confession. The only one that was distracting enough was P. Bradley Franklin. "What does the *P* stand for?" she blurted.

Bradley cocked an eyebrow as if he considered that a most improper question.

Annabelle was shocked at herself. She had made it a rule never to pry into other people's lives, and this was definitely prying. It was common knowledge that he never told anyone what the initial stood for. She knew she should be embarrassed at having been so forward, but she was beyond being embarrassed in front of him.

"Seems like it's only fair for you to tell me," she said in her defense. "I've told you my deepest, darkest secret. Apparently whatever the *P* in P. Bradley Franklin represents is your best-kept secret. No one seems to know what it stands for."

Bradley had to admit he liked her spunk. Unexpectedly he heard himself admitting, "It stands for Perceval."

Annabelle frowned thoughtfully. "The knight in King Arthur's court who sought the Holy Grail? If I recall my legends correctly, he was so pure of heart he was actually given a glimpse of the treasured object." She told herself that she had gone far enough, but she could not resist the urge to know more about the man sitting across from her. "And are you as pure of heart as your namesake?" she asked.

Bradley smiled quirkily. "I don't claim to be pure, but I try to be fair," he replied.

His smile caused a warm curling sensation in her abdomen, which was almost immediately followed by a wave of fear. Quickly she dropped her gaze to her food. "Fair is acceptable," she said, then concentrated on eating.

Bradley had seen the flash of warmth in her eyes. It had come close to being flirtatious, and he'd liked it. Then he'd seen the anxiousness. At least now he knew why she was nervous around him. It was only natural that her experience had left her with a fear of being alone with a man, especially one she didn't know well. An unexpected desire came over him to help Annabelle Royd get over this lingering fear. But he had no doubt that the only kind of relationship she would want with a man was a committed one, and he wasn't interested in being tied down to a career woman. When he did find someone to share his life with, it was going to be to a woman who wanted a home and family and nothing more. Someone else would have to help the lady.

"I'd appreciate it if you kept my secret," he said. "I lived through enough kidding for a lifetime when I was a child."

"Consider my lips sealed," she replied, experiencing a sudden wish that she could have been there to stand beside him as his friend. She scowled mentally. He wasn't interested in her as a friend or even as an acquaintance.

"And now, I'm going to work on my report until we're rescued," he said, rising from the table and carrying his dishes to the sink. He didn't like admitting it, but he wanted a diversion, something to get his mind off of her. She was definitely occupying too many of this thoughts.

Annabelle watched him. Just the way he moved caused a stirring of excitement within her, but it was always hampered by a dark shadow of fear. "I'll take care of cleaning up the breakfast things," she volunteered, as he began to wash the plate. It would give her something to do and at least keep her eyes off him, she reasoned.

Without protest, Bradley laid the dishrag aside and strode toward the coffee table in front of the fireplace where he'd set up his computer. The sooner he could get back to concentrating on his work, the better. Even though he knew it was the right thing to do, he found the thought of another man helping Annabelle get over her fear annoying. *I'm not the man for that job,* he told himself firmly as he sat in front of the machine and switched it on.

From where she was, Annabelle had an unobstructed view of Bradley, and it was tormenting. A part of her wanted to enjoy it, while another part drew back in apprehension. She took a final bite of egg, then rose and carried her dishes to the sink. With her back toward him, she could think more clearly. Her jaw firmed and determination glistened in her eyes. She would find a way to overcome this fear. She just wasn't certain how to go about it.

Chapter Six

Thursday came. Annabelle had avoided any contact with Bradley since their parting on Saturday afternoon. She told herself it was cowardly, but she was more comfortable not seeing him. *Of course it wouldn't have mattered if I'd crossed his path hourly,* she chided herself. *He'd never have noticed.*

As for the Swynites, they both apologized to her for the mix-up. They even bought the story about the mouse without a flicker of an eye. Edward did make a crack about having finally discovered something that could jar her out of her stoic disposition, but that was all. They adamantly refused to allow her to pay for the damages. She knew that Bradley had made the same offer and they'd refused him, too. Then they suggested that the entire episode was best forgotten, and it was never mentioned again.

Although she'd avoided Bradley, she hadn't been ignoring her promise to herself to do something about her lingering fear. On Sunday she'd gone to the local bookstore and purchased several of the newest books about rape and dealing with the crises that resulted. On Monday she'd gone to the library and found more. She'd been reading them vociferously.

The problem was that even though everything she read assured her that an intimate relationship could be exciting, stimulating and enjoyable, she could not rid herself of the nagging apprehension that persisted deep down inside. Even after eight years, although the intensity had faded some, she still recalled the physical pain and the feelings of degradation.

"It would seem that the only way to conquer this fear," she concluded as she stood at the window of her office looking out at the city skyline, "is to confront it." And the only way to do that would be to have a physical relationship with a man. This thought shook her to the bone. But she wanted a full life; she wanted to look to the promises of the future and not be constrained by the dark shadows of the past.

The problem now was to find the right man. "He would have to be someone I'm attracted to." P. Bradley Franklin's image filled her mind. "Don't be ridiculous," she scoffed at herself. He considered her about as alluring as a toad.

A smile played at the corners of her mouth. In the fairy tales it was always the prince who was the toad and the princess who changed him back. But in her case, the roles were reversed. "I'm the toad," she mused. "And I need to find myself a prince of a man

who will help me become a whole human again." Or
a knight in shining armor. This thought brought back
her frown. Perceval Bradley Franklin did not want to
be her knight in shining armor.

The buzzer on her desk sounded, and she glanced at
her watch. She gave her shoulders a healthy shrug as
if that would shake off these personal concerns.
"Time to get my mind back to work," she ordered
herself as she punched the intercom button.

"You asked me to buzz you when it was time for the
board meeting," Mary James, Annabelle's secretary,
said from the other end.

"Thanks," she replied. She drew a nervous breath.
Through the years, she'd met the various members of
the board, but she'd never been invited to a formal
meeting. The truth was, she wasn't really sure why
she'd been included today.

Bradley's report had been given to all the members
yesterday so that they would have time to read it before today's gathering. "Maybe Randall is so sure of
Edward's appointment as president he wants me there
to introduce me as the new vice president of marketing," she speculated aloud. This thought should have
brought a rush of excitement, but it didn't. She
breathed a tired sigh. After eight years of concentrating on her career, suddenly it had become her second
priority. She wasn't certain if she should thank Perceval Bradley Franklin or curse him. "However, at the
moment, I don't have time to decide," she said. Again
ordering the thoughts about her personal life out of
her mind, she strode from her office and into the conference room.

Bradley and the board members, other than the Swynites, looked surprised to see her enter.

"I've asked Ms. Royd to join us," Randall said, motioning for Annabelle to take a seat in a chair in the corner of the room.

As she sat down, she glanced toward Bradley. His expression was cool and impersonal as if they were total strangers. It was as if the night at the cabin had never happened. As if they'd never shared secrets. Which was just as well, she told herself. P. Bradley Franklin would be gone by this afternoon and she'd probably never see him again. And that was fine with her, she told herself for the hundredth time.

Bradley's gaze traveled over the board members, resting momentarily on Randall and Edward. When Annabelle had entered the room, he'd instinctively sensed trouble brewing. Or maybe he was simply overreacting to her. She did have a way of setting his nerves on edge. He didn't like admitting it, but he'd been avoiding her since the weekend. Every time he saw her, he had a strong urge to try to help her get over her fear of men. But he kept pointing out to himself that this urge was irrational, and would be unfair to her if he should attempt to act on it.

Randall tapped his gavel to bring the meeting to order. "I've read through Mr. Franklin's report," he began, his expression stern. "Although he couched it in the most diplomatic terms, pointing out that today businesses do need people with innovative ideas in order to grow and compete, I resent the implication that Edward needs to be kept in harness. And while we here at Swynite Industries greatly value Ms. Royd's abilities, I further resent the implication that the smooth running of the marketing department can be attributed to her rather than my son."

Annabelle blinked in shocked surprise.

"The report merely says that your son showed good managerial sense in assigning associates tasks at which they were proficient," Howard Zyle pointed out. "The report didn't say he couldn't handle the tasks himself." A baiting quality entered his voice. "However, your interpretation might imply that you believe that to be the case."

Randall snorted, and his shoulders squared. He rose and placed the palms of his hands flat on the table. Then he leaned toward Howard Zyle, his expression one of controlled fury. "I have complete confidence in my son's abilities. However, I'm not a fool, Howard. I know you like to read between the lines and interpret what is there to your advantage. And I know that you want your own man in as president." He drew a deep breath, straightened, then reseated himself. He let his gaze wander over the faces of the men at the table, claiming their undivided attention. "Therefore, I feel I must bring my own perspective to this meeting."

On the outside Bradley maintained a poised but relaxed posture. Inside he prepared for trouble. He'd come up against strong adversaries before, and he didn't doubt for one moment that Randall Swynite would be one of the strongest. An ugly suspicion began to form in his mind.

Out of the corner of his eye, Randall glanced toward Annabelle. She recognized that look. It was the one he always got when he had some little trick up his sleeve that was going to win him what he wanted. Suddenly her guard was up. She didn't know what he planned, but she knew she was the pawn in his game.

"I feel that Mr. Franklin's fairness has been compromised," Randall went on. There was accusation in his voice and on his face as he focused his full attention on Annabelle. "Last weekend, there was a scheduling mistake. As a result Ms. Royd and Mr. Franklin spent a night alone together at my mountain retreat. It is my contention that Ms. Royd, who has made it very clear she wants my son's position as VP of marketing, used that opportunity to further her career."

Annabelle flushed scarlet. "That's not true!" she said, rising indignantly to her feet.

Ignoring her, Randall turned to Bradley. "And I further contend that this report is a reflection of your lust, rather than a fair evaluation of my son's abilities."

"Personally, I think you're miffed because Bradley's report suggests *you* haven't been running the company as productively as you should," Howard Zyle interjected, his tone carrying a challenge.

Randall shot him a deadly look. "That, I feel, can also be attributed to Ms. Royd." He again turned toward Annabelle. His expression was one of a father greatly disappointed by an offspring. "My son and I took her in and taught her all we know about running this business, and this is the way she repays us."

"That's not true!" Annabelle repeated, unable to think of anything else to say. Bile rose in her throat.

Her reputation was being unfairly threatened once again, and she felt as helpless as she had the first time.

Howard Zyle regarded Randall with dry amusement. "Seems more likely to me that you, your son and Ms. Royd working together arranged the secluded weekend for her and Bradley. Only your plan backfired when she used it to her advantage."

Annabelle's hands balled into fists at her sides. *"No!"* she protested sharply. Howard and Randall were glaring at one another, but the other members of the board were studying her speculatively. They looked as if they were seeing her for the first time, and she knew they believed she'd been intimate with Bradley. Hot tears burned at the back of her eyes, but she refused to cry. Instead, she stood straight and tall and faced them with dignity. "I did nothing..."

Bradley had had occasion to think on his feet before, but never this fast. The business he'd spent years building was being threatened. No one would hire him if they thought he could be seduced into falsifying a report. And then there was Ms. Royd. He was surprised by the strength of his desire to protect her. *I'm concerned for her because she's lived through enough anguish, and she doesn't deserve this kind of treatment,* he reasoned. A solution presented itself. It was radical, he admitted. But at the moment, it was the only one he could come up with. Rising, he moved toward Annabelle. "Darling, I'm sorry," he said gruffly.

Annabelle stared at him in disbelief. Had he lost his mind? All eyes in the room were on them now. The shock she was feeling was reflected on Randall's and

Edward's faces. She stood frozen, wondering what in the world could possibly happen next.

Reaching her in three long strides, Bradley captured her by the shoulders. Using his body to block her from the view of the others, he leaned close and whispered, "Just follow my lead and I'll get us both out of this."

There was a command in his eyes for her to trust him. What choice did she have? she thought. Then, to her surprise, she realized that she *did* trust him. She gave a small nod of agreement.

He dropped a light kiss on her lips. Then releasing her, he turned back toward the men at the table.

Annabelle knew the kiss had only been for show, a part of the gambit he'd devised, but the warmth of it lingered. When he slid his arm around her shoulders she felt like a maiden in distress being rescued by a knight. My mind is going to mush, she thought frantically, ridiculing these reactions. Sternly she commanded herself to keep a rational perspective.

"I admit to having very strong feelings for Ms. Royd...." Bradley paused. "Annie," he corrected, choosing a pet name for her to give his story more authenticity. "However, neither she nor I had any intention of using this report to further her career here at Swynite Industries. She was, in fact, planning to hand in her resignation this afternoon. We're going to be married, and I want her with me." He met Randall's stunned gaze with cold reserve. "As for my report, it's a fair and accurate assessment, and I stand by it." His gaze traveled over the other men in the room. "Now I'm going to help Annie pack. I won't allow her to remain here another day with men who show her so little respect. If there are any questions about my report you'll find me in her office. Good day, gentlemen." And with that he took Annabelle's arm and urged her toward the door.

The fact that not only was she not a vice president but that she was out of a job barely registered in Annabelle's mind. The word *married* dominated all her thoughts as she allowed him to guide her out of the conference room and down the hall to her office. Excitement mingled with apprehension. *You don't actually expect him to go through with a marriage,* she chided herself. *Of course not,* came the reply. She laughed at herself for even considering the possibility, and the muddle of emotions the thought of being married to him had caused died a swift death.

As they entered her office, he released her, then locked the door. Once their privacy was assured, he strode to the window and stood looking out. He was still finding it a little hard to believe he'd gotten himself into this mess. And why had marriage occurred to him? Surely he could have thought of a better solution. Out of the frying pan and into the fire, he mused.

"Now what do we do?" Annabelle asked, too tense to remain silent.

He turned toward her. "We plan the wedding. I'd prefer it to be small. Maybe only immediate family. But whatever you want is fine with me. I'll pay for everything."

Annabelle blinked. "You can't be serious," she blurted, unable to believe he actually meant to go through with it.

He frowned impatiently. She was looking at him as if she thought he'd lost his mind. Well, that thought had occurred to him, too. "I don't see that we have a choice," he replied tersely. "Both our reputations are on the line. No one's going to hire me if they think I can be manipulated by a pretty woman. As for you, wherever you go, they'll want letters of recommendation, and they'll ask Randall for one. He could seriously damage your career opportunities. And even if he doesn't make any allusion in writing to his claim that you seduced me, there will be rumors, and there will be men who will want to see if there is any truth to those rumors." This last thought brought a bitter taste to his mouth as he suddenly pictured some less ethical types attempting to take advantage of her.

Annabelle had to admit his reasoning was valid. However, she was certain he didn't honestly want to marry her, and she had her pride. "Don't you think marriage is a little drastic?" she said, determined to offer him a way out of this.

"This situation calls for drastic measures," he replied. But surely he could have come up with another solution, he added to himself, again racking his brain. But nothing occurred to him. "It's not unusual for marriages to be short-lived in this day and age," he reasoned aloud. "We'll get married. Then after a couple of years we can get a quiet divorce."

Annabelle reminded herself that just that morning she'd concluded that she needed to face having a physical relationship with a man. And marriage suited her much better than an affair. But she hated that he felt trapped into marrying her. Hardly the kind of atmosphere she had hoped to have surrounding her venture into intimacy. "Maybe we could just have a long engagement," she suggested.

Bradley considered the possibility. But another ugly thought nagged at him. "There's the broken door lock to consider," he said grimly. "If Randall let that little fact be known, it could lead to speculation that I forced myself on you and the report was my way of buying your silence."

A cold chill ran through Annabelle. A rumor like that could seriously harm Bradley. She didn't want to see that happen. He'd treated her fairly and he deserved to be treated fairly in return. "Randall can be vindictive when he doesn't get his way," she admitted. Still she hesitated. She'd always thought that when she did marry, it would be to someone she loved and who loved her back.

Bradley knew it wasn't rational, but her hesitation to marry him stung. Then he mentally kicked himself as the reason for her reluctance dawned on him. "You don't have to worry about my making any...demands on you. We'll have separate bedrooms." Attempting to point out a positive side, he added, "I'll teach you my business. I can use a good assistant. Then after our divorce you can go into business for yourself, be your own boss. You won't have to put up with the Swynites of this world."

While I'm entertaining all sorts of romantic notions, he's outlining a business arrangement, she mused. She felt like an idiot. Well, at least she wouldn't have to spend any sleepless nights worrying about consummating their vows. This thought was supposed to bring a measure of relief. Instead, she felt a twinge of insult. *Not insult,* she corrected. *I knew he wasn't attracted to me.* It was a twinge of regret. She had been hoping to use this opportunity to overcome her fear. Suddenly another thought occurred to her. "I won't be made a laughingstock by having a husband who has affairs."

Bradley scowled. This was getting complicated. "All right. I've worked too hard to get to where I am today to start rebuilding all over again. I can survive on cold showers for a couple of years."

This time she *definitely* felt insulted. She knew she hadn't encouraged him to think of her as a woman. She would also have accepted his standoffishness without being offended if she'd thought it was due to his concern for her feelings about her past. She would even have been pleased that he was so thoughtful. But that wasn't the impression he gave. What he exhibited was a total indifference toward her. Well, if he preferred cold showers, he could have his cold showers.

"Then," she said, "you now have a fiancée and a new business associate."

Bradley held out his hand. "Good."

As she reached out to accept the handshake to cement their deal, Annabelle wondered how many people confirmed their engagement in this businesslike manner. Then his hand closed around hers and a warmth spread up her arm. A fire kindled within her. Along with it came the fear, but the fire continued to burn. She wanted to scream in frustration. He may not be the only one taking cold showers, she thought.

Bradley was surprised by the warmth of her touch. He suddenly found himself picturing Annabelle in her jeans and sweater with her hair hanging in wild disarray. The image aroused him. Forcefully he pushed it out of his mind. Annabelle not only would require a permanent commitment but she deserved it, he told himself sternly. And he wasn't prepared to give her that. She wasn't the kind of woman he wanted for a wife. He wanted a domestically minded female. Annabelle was definitely career-minded. "I'll go find some boxes," he said, releasing her hand. "We'll have you packed and out of here tonight."

"But..." She started to protest, to say that she couldn't just leave. There were business matters that should be cleared up. Then she remembered what the Swynites had tried to do to her. They didn't deserve her consideration. "That sounds like a good idea," she agreed.

Still, after Bradley had left she called in Dick Jarvis. She considered him the most competent of the people she worked with on a daily basis. When Bradley came back he found her going over current files with the man. "I hate leaving loose ends," she said in answer to his questioning glance. "Besides, this company doesn't belong just to the Swynites. There are other investors to consider."

Bradley had to admit he admired her dedication to her job. He had no doubt that she would be an excellent business associate. But a wife? He was still finding it difficult to accept the situation he'd gotten himself into.

"Dick has worked with me on several of these projects," she said, as Bradley put down the boxes he'd found and approached her desk. "This should only take a couple of hours. But there's no reason for you to stick around."

"I think I should stay just in case the board decides to consult me about my report," he replied. "Besides, I wouldn't consider leaving you here with those two snakes." Startled that he honestly felt that way, he reminded himself that Annabelle could take care of herself just fine. He had the bruises to prove it.

Annabelle glanced at him. The protectiveness she'd heard in his voice sparked a warmth within her. *Don't be a fool,* she admonished herself. He was only putting on a show for Dick. Without thinking, she heard herself saying, "Living up to your name?"

Bradley raised a cautioning eyebrow.

Annabelle knew she shouldn't have made the crack about his first name. She grimaced and glanced toward him with silent apology. Then she gave a shrug in Dick's direction as if to say, "Don't pay any attention to me. I don't know what I'm saying at the moment." To her relief, Dick nodded with understanding.

The way her nose crinkled when she grimaced that way, made her look downright kissable, Bradley thought, then scowled. *Thinking like that will get you into trouble,* he warned himself. Turning away, he found a magazine, then took a seat across the room.

Annabelle was not happy. She had to stop letting her emotions take control. *Think business relationship,* she ordered herself. *Think salvaging your career.* Having had this little talk with herself, she forced her full concentration onto the files she was going over with Dick.

Bradley attempted to ignore their presence. He needed to think this whole situation through clearly and analytically. But as hard as he tried not to, he found himself glancing covertly at Annabelle. He noticed that the man working beside her was sitting so close that every once in a while their shoulders would touch. This irritated him. He recalled that she'd always kept a distance between him and her. *Except for that kick that nearly broke a couple of my ribs,* he corrected. That she didn't seem uneasy around this Dick person also irritated him. After discovering the reason behind her nightmare, he'd assumed that she was uneasy around all men. *But apparently it's my particular presence that displeases Ms. Royd,* he mused. That was going to make this marriage business even more difficult. He turned his attention back to his magazine. Again he wondered how he'd gotten himself into this mess.

Annabelle had finished going over the last of her current projects with Dick. He left, and she was beginning to pack her personal effects when a knock on her office door was immediately followed by Howard Zyle's entrance.

"Thought you two might like to know how the board meeting is going," he said. "But first I want to apologize for Randall's behavior. It was in very poor taste." The hint of a smile played at one corner of his mouth. "He hates losing." The hint became a full smile. "Truth is, Edward would probably have gotten the presidency without any trouble if Randall had kept his mouth shut. No one else interpreted the report as critically as he did. I admit we're a conservative bunch, but we're businessmen. We know there have to be changes. Randall's the one who's fought new ideas all these years." He shook his head as if condemning Randall. "Anyway, Edward did some fancy apologizing for his father's behavior, and the board relented and voted him in."

"So much for considering a man's ethics," Annabelle muttered.

Howard frowned. "The board got around that by laying the full blame for Randall's accusations on Randall. Edward claimed no prior knowledge of what his father intended to say at the meeting, and the others decided to buy it. But I'll remember not to turn my back on either of them in the future." He extended his hand toward Bradley. "Your report was thorough and fair. You'll get an excellent letter of recommendation from me personally and the board as a whole."

Bradley accepted the handshake. "I appreciate that."

Howard turned to Annabelle. "Under the circumstances, I'm sorry to see you leaving. You were always excellent at your job, and while I felt hindered by it, I admired your loyalty toward the Swynites. I'd like to have had you remain here with that loyalty shifted to me." He extended a hand toward Annabelle. "Good luck. I'll write you an excellent letter of recommendation for your file and see that the board follows suit."

Annabelle accepted the handshake. "Thank you," she said as she marveled at how, in just a few short hours, alliances could be so quickly changed. She had thought that the Swynites were her allies. Now they had proved to be foes, and it was Howard Zyle who was on her side.

Howard's gaze shifted from Annabelle to Bradley. "I know that engagements are tenuous these days." He frowned musingly. "My daughter's been engaged half a dozen times but never made it to the altar." The musing quality disappeared and his expression became stern. "But in your case, there'll be people watching. I'd suggest neither of you let premarital jitters thwart your plans."

It was clear to Annabelle that Howard suspected this marriage might be a ploy; he was warning them that they'd better play it out. Bradley was right. They had no choice if they wanted to insure that neither of their reputations was blemished by rumors and innuendos.

They were interrupted by a knock, followed by Edward's entrance. "Come to give the couple a bit of sage advice, Howard?" he asked with the broad grin of a man who was pleased with the world.

"Just my congratulations," Howard replied, then added pointedly, "and an apology from myself and the board for your father's attempt to smear their reputations."

Edward's expression immediately became serious. "Precisely why I'm here, too." He turned to Annabelle. "I deeply regret the things my father said, and I wish you and Bradley all the best."

His gaze shifted to Bradley, and although he continued to smile, the smile didn't reach his eyes. Instead he studied Bradley speculatively. "I do have to admit you two surprised me. I could have sworn you were avoiding each other these past few days."

Outwardly, Annabelle showed no reaction. Inwardly, a knot formed in her stomach. She'd thought that it was just luck that she'd been so successful in avoiding Bradley since the weekend. It hadn't occurred to her that he might be attempting to avoid her, also. He must hate the idea of having to marry her, she thought, and the knot tightened.

"We didn't want our romance to become office gossip," Bradley replied, slipping an arm around Annabelle's shoulders. "We're both very private people."

Edward frowned thoughtfully, then he nodded as if accepting this explanation. "Well, good luck to both of you." He extended his hand toward Bradley. "I hope you'll accept my apology."

Bradley scowled at Edward's hand. "I don't like what your father tried to do. It'll take a while before I'm ready to forgive it." A warning entered his voice. "In the meantime, I'd better not hear even the slightest hint of any unpleasant rumors about either myself or Annie."

Annabelle saw the flash of fear in Edward's eyes. He held up his hand in a sign of peace. "Ann was an excellent employee. Exemplary, in fact. And you were a professional to the core. That's all anyone will ever hear from me."

"Good," Bradley replied.

"I think it's time for us to be getting back to the board meeting," Howard said, giving Edward a tap on the shoulder.

"Yes," Edward agreed quickly.

As the door closed behind them, Annabelle sighed heavily. "Do the bad guys always win?"

Dropping his arm from her shoulders, Bradley caught her by the chin and tilted her face upward. He regarded her with a patronizing frown. "Two days ago you thought Howard was the bad guy. What makes you think he's suddenly the good guy?"

"You're right," she conceded. Disillusionment entered her eyes. "Maybe there are no good guys."

Bradley scowled. "I'm a good guy."

"And you just got tangled in a web you can't get out of," she replied.

"*We* are tangled in a web," he corrected. An expression of grim determination spread over his features. "But we'll get out of it together."

Chapter Seven

"Engaged? My big sister, the career woman of the century, is engaged?" Linda Justin shifted her gaze from Annabelle to Bradley then back to Annabelle. "This *is* a surprise!" The stunned expression on her face changed to a wide grin. "This is great!" Suddenly springing into motion, she gave Bradley a hug. "Welcome to the family."

No two sisters could be more different, Bradley thought as he accepted the hug. To begin with, there was scarcely any physical resemblance. Linda was short with an hourglass figure. Her hair was blond, her eyes blue and her face was pretty in a cute way, with deep dimples when she smiled. Her daughters resembled her markedly. Then there was Linda's outgoing personality. Unlike Annabelle, she smiled a lot, and the smile was usually accompanied by a giggle or two.

As soon as Linda released Bradley, Frank, her husband, extended his hand toward his wife's future brother-in-law. Bradley had guessed Linda was in her mid-twenties. Frank, he decided, was three or four years older. The man stood around five foot eleven, Bradley judged, and had a more somber presence than his wife. It was also clear that the third triplet, Jack, took after his father; he had the same dark hair and gray eyes. Frank was lean, with an angular face, and at the moment he was regarding Bradley with a smile that didn't quite reach his eyes. Instead, they held a warning. "I think real highly of Ann," he said. "I want her to be happy."

"I want that, too," Bradley replied, and was surprised by how much he meant it. He made a promise to himself that he'd see that she came out of this experience without any lingering scars.

Frank nodded his approval and now his smile reached his eyes. "Then welcome to the family."

Linda drew a relieved breath and cast her husband an "I can't believe you did that" glance. "You have to excuse Frank," she said. "He's the closet thing Ann has to a big brother, and he takes his responsibilities seriously."

Annabelle had been watching nervously. Because her sister and brother-in-law lived next door, they'd been the logical ones to tell first. Besides, it hadn't been left up to her. When she had pulled into her driveway with Bradley following in his car, Frank had just gotten home from work. Linda had come out to greet him, seen Annabelle and Bradley, waved and started toward them. Frank had followed. Annabelle knew they were probably surprised to see her with a man. They'd both been trying to get her to date more. Still uncertain that Bradley meant to go through with this marriage, she'd glanced at him questioningly. But the moment she'd introduced Frank and Linda as her sister and brother-in-law, Bradley had introduced himself as her fiancé. She'd expected them to be stunned. But she was a little surprised by Frank's sudden big-brother manner. She was even more surprised by the sound of sincerity in Bradley's voice when he responded. *He just meant he wants us both to come out of this smelling like roses,* she reasoned, refusing to believe for a moment that he felt any deep personal concern for her.

"I'm glad Annie has people who care so much about her," Bradley said, his tone assuring Linda he'd taken no offense.

Annabelle tensed slightly. Normally she hated being called Annie. She preferred Ann or Annabelle. Annie had always seemed so childish. But it didn't sound childish when Bradley said it. In fact she sort of liked it. *My mind really is in a muddle,* she thought.

Linda was beaming again. "I still can't believe this. Ann falling in love at first sight."

A fresh wave of nervousness washed over Annabelle. It would never have been noticed by anyone who didn't know her extremely well, but there was the vaguest hint of uncertainty in Linda's eyes. The last thing Annabelle wanted was for her sister to question the engagement.

"It happened to you," she reminded Linda quickly. A crooked smile suddenly tilted one corner of her mouth as she glanced toward Frank and remembered her sister's first encounter with the man. Glad to be able to shift the focus of the conversation to someone else, she turned to Bradley. "Linda had come to spend the summer with me. Frank lived next door, a lonely bachelor—"

"But a happy one," Frank interjected playfully, and received a jab in the ribs from Linda.

"Lonely but happy," Annabelle amended. "Anyway, the first day Linda was here she got into some sort of dispute with him over a cat on his roof. It ended with him climbing up to rescue the animal."

"That didn't need rescuing in the first place, as I had been trying to explain to this cute little blonde." Cupping Linda's chin in his hand, he looked down into her cherublike face. "Who would have thought that someone who seemed so gentle could be so tough?" Shaking his head as if still bewildered by his wife, he turned back to Bradley. "Anyway, she ended up forcing me to go up on the roof to rescue the little beast."

Linda looked sheepish. "Only he was right. The cat didn't need rescuing. It ran away from him and got down on its own. Only Frank couldn't get down."

"I hate heights," Frank admitted self-consciously.

Linda grinned. "So I had to go up and save him. His male pride had been wounded, and he was furious with me."

"But my sister," Annabelle said, picking up the story, "decided right then and there that he was the man for her. Frank never had a chance."

"If I'd known what she was thinking, I'd probably have packed my bags and run," Frank said gruffly. "But as it was, I was caught, hook, line and sinker, before I even knew what was happening." He placed his arm affectionately around his wife's shoulders. "And I've never regretted it for a moment."

"He's just happy to have a wife who'll go up on a ladder and clean out the gutters for him," Linda kidded.

Watching and listening to them, Annabelle envied them. She'd hoped to have this same kind of loving, happy relationship with the man she married. *And I will,* she assured herself. *I just won't have it with this marriage, because this isn't the real thing, except on a piece of paper.*

"Look, why don't I take a couple more steaks out of the freezer and you two join us for dinner?" Linda said, freeing herself from her husband and hooking an arm through Bradley's. "I'd like to get to know my new brother-in-law a little better."

"We really can't." Bradley smiled down at the blonde as he disentangled his arm. It occurred to him that even if Frank had packed his bags and moved to Alaska, Linda would've caught up with him and gotten him. She had that kind of determination. But he and Annabelle had business to take care of that couldn't wait, and no amount of determination on Linda's part could change that. "I've got to leave town tomorrow to take care of some business matters, and Annie and I have some plans to make before I go."

"Oh, sure," Linda replied, her disappointment clear on her face.

"I remember when we had plans to make and we didn't want any company," Frank reminded her.

Linda flushed and her smile returned. "I'll see you tomorrow," she said to Annabelle, her tone firm. Turning to Bradley, she gave him another hug, adding, "And, again, welcome to the family."

Annabelle breathed a sigh of relief a few minutes later as she and Bradley entered her kitchen. Linda and Frank had accepted the news with fewer questions than she'd expected. However, she suspected that tomorrow would be different. Linda had probably already come up with at least a dozen things to ask. "I'm sorry about Frank's big-brother routine," she said turning to face Bradley.

"That was nothing," he assured her, then grimaced. "You're going to have to face my sister."

"I don't think I like the sound of that," Annabelle replied, her nervousness multiplying. It hadn't been until she'd seen Frank and Linda that it had dawned on her that marriage would bring the families into this farce.

A mischievous glimmer suddenly shone in Bradley's eyes. "Don't worry. She wants me married. She thinks it will improve me. I'll tell her that if she pesters you too much you'll leave me standing at the altar. That should hold her at bay."

Annabelle tried to smile, but she was too tense. "I suppose we do have to go through with this," she said anxiously.

The amusement left Bradley's eyes. She couldn't feel any more trapped than he did. "Zyle made that clear," he said. His manner becoming brisk, he took a small notebook out of his pocket. "As I told Linda, I have to leave tonight. I've got an eight-o'clock flight to Kansas City. I've got an early appointment scheduled there for tomorrow morning that I can't miss. It's about a job I contracted for months ago. It can't be put off. I'll have to leave the plans for the wedding up to you. I figure the sooner we get married, the sooner we can get divorced. How about if we schedule the ceremony for a week from this coming Saturday?"

"Fine," Annabelle agreed, none of this seeming truly real.

"Is a small wedding, just family, okay with you?" Bradley asked in the same businesslike tones.

"I think that would be best," she replied, wanting to involve as few people in this as possible.

"I thought we'd have it here in Pittsburgh. That will make it easier for you to plan," he continued, beginning to jot down notes. "I'll pay for everything. We'll fly your parents, my parents and my sister and her family in." He paused and glanced at her worriedly. "Are your parents okay with flying? I know there's a lot of people who aren't."

"They don't mind flying," she heard herself saying, feeling more and more like she was caught up in a weird, fast-paced dream.

"Good." He paused, then continued, "You'll have to make reservations for a rehearsal dinner and a reception." He frowned. "Where do you want to have this wedding? Church? Chapel? Office of the Justice of the Peace, if they do it that way here in Pennsylvania?"

Annabelle held her hands up. "I need some time to think."

Bradley nodded. Closing the notebook, he stuck it back into his pocket. "I'll leave the arrangements up to you. Just let me know where I have to be and when."

"Where and when," Annabelle repeated.

Bradley was watching her. She looked slightly panicked. "We'll get through this," he assured her.

Annabelle took a deep, calming breath. "I know." Anger abruptly etched itself into her features, as her mind flashed back to the boardroom. "I still can't believe Randall did this to me...to us. Men!" she seethed.

The next couple of years were going to be rocky, Bradley thought, reading the ire in her eyes. He glanced at his watch. "I've got to be leaving for the airport. I'll call you tomorrow. You can let me know when I have to be here to get our license." Opening his briefcase, he took out his checkbook and scribbled out a check. "This should cover the expenses for now," he said, handing it to her.

Annabelle blinked as she glanced at the amount. It was made out for four thousand dollars.

"You probably should walk me out," he suggested.

Setting the check aside, she followed him to the front door. He paused long enough to allow her to catch up with him, then they walked side by side to his car. "Got an audience," he warned in a whisper, looking past her toward Linda and Frank's house as they came to a halt by the driver's door. "I'll call," he said in louder tones. Then he dropped a light kiss on her lips before climbing in behind the wheel. As he started the engine, he determinedly pushed the thoughts of how sweet she tasted out of his mind. That was not part of the deal.

The feel of his lips lingered warmly on hers as Annabelle watched him drive away. "But there's nothing to get excited about," she muttered. "He only did it for show."

She'd barely reached her front door when Linda came jogging across the lawn. "I couldn't wait until tomorrow," she said, following Annabelle inside.

"Shouldn't you be feeding Frank?" Annabelle asked, still feeling shaken and wanting a little more time to sort out her thoughts before facing her sister.

"He's perfectly capable of feeding himself," Linda replied. "And the triplets are already fed and ready to be played with as soon as he's done. So I've got at least two hours of freedom." She frowned worriedly as she followed Annabelle into the kitchen and watched her sister take a couple of aspirin. "For someone who just got engaged, you don't seem too happy."

Annabelle forced a smile. "I am," she said firmly. She didn't like lying to Linda. But Linda was the kind of open personality whose feelings were reflected like a mirror on her face. If she knew the truth, her concern would be blatantly evident. That would cause Annabelle's parents to be worried. And Linda was not good at keeping secrets. She was bound to tell Frank. He might understand why Annabelle and Bradley were doing this, but he wouldn't approve. Her parents might even be able to get the truth out of Linda. That could cause even more tension. This wedding was supposed to be a festive, happy affair, not a wake. She would tell Linda the truth later, but not now. "It's just been a long, very eventful day, and I'm exhausted."

Linda didn't look convinced. "I was under the impression that you and P. Bradley Franklin weren't on the best of terms. Whenever his name has come up during the past week, you've acted more nervous than excited."

"I was nervous. I've never been in love before." Annabelle congratulated herself. This wasn't a real lie. She had never been in love before, and she wasn't actually admitting that she was now. Her phrasing only implied it.

"Love can have an unnerving effect on people," Linda conceded. Her mouth formed a thoughtful pout. "But I have to admit I never expected anything so sudden from you. I sort of pictured you going with a man for maybe six months or so before you even admitted to being serious."

"So did I," Annabelle conceded. "This has all come as as much of a surprise to me as it has to you." Again she congratulated herself for not having to lie.

"I suppose you plan a long engagement?" Linda said, clearly still trying to make some sense of all this.

Annabelle forced more cheerfulness into her voice. "Actually, we're planning on getting married a week from this coming Saturday."

Linda's eyes rounded in disbelief. "A week from this coming Saturday?"

Annabelle had braced herself for this reaction. "Bradley has a very busy schedule," she said with a calmness that surprised even her. "Besides, now that we've made the decision, we don't see any reason to wait."

"But that doesn't give you any time to plan a wedding," Linda protested. "You've always been conservative, the one who thought out your moves before you made them. I know I've scolded you at times for being too serious, too contemplative. But this time you're moving too fast even for me. You only met Bradley a week ago."

"You always said that one day a man would come along who would sweep me off my feet," Annabelle reminded her.

"I know," Linda replied. "But I didn't expect him to sweep you up and carry you away in one swish."

Annabelle wished she could confide in Linda right this minute. But her instincts warned her that wouldn't be wise. Besides, knowing the truth would not diminish Linda's worry. So, instead, Annabelle gave her sister a hug. "I appreciate your concern. But don't worry. I know what I'm doing."

Linda returned the hug. "You've always shown good sense in the past," she admitted. Still she looked skeptical. "What about your job? Where does Bradley live? Is he willing to move here?"

"We haven't settled our living arrangements yet," Annabelle replied. "But I've quit my job. I'm going to work for him."

Shock returned to Linda's face. "You've quit your job? You were in line for a vice presidency!"

"Things change." And these questions were getting harder and harder to field, Annabelle thought tiredly. She decided on a new tack. "I want this," she said firmly. "And I need your support. I don't want Mom and Dad worrying about me. I want them to be happy for me, and that will mean you have to be happy for me and not question my decision."

For a long moment, Linda regarded her in silence, then she said with resignation, "Frank says he's never known anyone as levelheaded as you, and I know I never have. If you honestly believe this will make you happy, then I want it for you, too."

Annabelle breathed a relieved sigh. "Thanks."

"Just remember that, if this doesn't work out the way you want, I love you and I'll be here for you, and so will Frank and the triplets," Linda declared, giving Annabelle another hug.

"I appreciate that," Annabelle replied, "but you really don't have to worry."

"Worrying is what sisters are for," Linda returned with a loving smile.

"That's what Mom says moms are for," Annabelle reminded her. Then she grimaced. "And I guess I'd better call her and tell her the news. Bradley wants them to fly up for the wedding." She looked beseechingly at her sister. "And I want you to tell them you think this marriage is going to be great."

"All right," Linda agreed, but she still looked skeptical.

Later that night, lying in bed, Annabelle stared into the darkness. Her parents had been as shocked as Linda, but Linda's assurances had helped. They were going to fly in for the wedding. "And that takes care of my family." Her jaw tensed with purpose. "Tomorrow I'll begin making the arrangements."

As she drifted off to sleep, Bradley's image filled her mind, and she wondered how his family was taking the news.

Several hundred miles away, Bradley sat in his hotel room. "This has definitely been one of the more eventful days of my life," he muttered.

He looked at his watch. His parents lived in Maine. It was too late to call them. But it wasn't too late to call his sister in California. "Might as well get it over with," he ordered himself. Two minutes later, Helen was on the line.

"This is a surprise, big brother," she said. He heard the concern in her voice. In his mind's eye, he pictured her. Her long, sun-bleached blond hair was probably pulled back into a ponytail or some other casual style. She was tall, five ten to be exact, and slender like a model. Her pretty face would be screwed up into a look of worry, which would wrinkle her freckled nose and darken the blue of her eyes slightly. "You don't usually call me in the middle of the week." Reprimand entered her voice. "In fact, you haven't called in nearly two months."

"Sorry, but I've been busy," he replied.

"You're forgiven," came her response, the reprimand gone and the concern back. "What's going on? And don't try to lie to me. I know you too well. You sound worried."

Bradley frowned. He'd meant to keep his tone light. "I'm just tired," he replied levelly, then forced enthusiasm into his voice. "But I wanted to call you as soon as possible. I'm getting married."

"I don't believe it!" Helen laughed. "My big brother is getting married." She laughed again. "So that's what's been keeping you so busy these past two months."

Bradley considered letting her continue to believe this, but she was certain to find out the truth when she came to the wedding. "Actually, I haven't known Annie quite that long," he hedged, then continued quickly, "But you know me, when I make a decision, I like to act on it as quickly as possible. The wedding is going to be in Pittsburgh a week from Saturday. I want you and John and the kids to come." Quickly he outlined his plans for their airline tickets and hotel rooms.

"A week from Saturday?" Helen repeated. Suddenly her tone became businesslike. "What's this woman's name and phone number? I should call her and ask if there is anything I can do to help with the arrangements."

He loved his sister, but he also knew she could be a persistent busybody when the mood struck her. "You're too far away to help with anything," he pointed out, barely able to keep himself from adding an order for her not to call. He was amazed at how much he wanted to protect Annabelle from Helen's probing. Ms. Royd could take care of herself. Of that he was certain. *I just don't want anyone rocking the boat,* he reasoned.

A suspicious note entered Helen's voice. "I'm getting the feeling you don't want me to talk to this person you're considering marrying."

"I'm not *considering* marrying her," he corrected, his jaw set in a resolute line. It didn't matter that Annabelle didn't want to marry him and he didn't want to marry her. For the sake of both their futures, the ceremony was going to take place. "I *am* marrying her," he finished.

"Then as your sister, it's only polite that I call her and offer my congratulations," Helen insisted.

Bradley knew he was waging a losing battle. Besides, Helen would be meeting Annabelle at the wedding. They might as well get over the first awkward confrontation ahead of time. "All right. I'll give you her name and number, but I want your word you won't put her through your usual third degree."

Helen issued a gasp of indignation. "Me? Sweet, little ol' me?"

"Yes, sweet little ol' you," Bradley replied. "I can't remember how many of my dates told me never to call them again unless I became an only child."

Mock innocence entered Helen's voice. "Any woman who can't stand up to me would be no match for you. I was saving you from boredom."

"Did it ever occur to you that I might like a woman who is quiet, a little shy and unassuming?"

Helen groaned. "Don't tell me you're engaged to a mouse? It won't last. You only *think* you want a meek, subservient female. You'll walk all over her like a doormat."

Annabelle's image entered Bradley's mind. She was no mouse. "No, I'm not engaged to a meek, subservient female," he assured his sister. "The truth is, she's a match even for you."

"Now I feel better. It's obvious you admire her," Helen said, the worry in her voice fading.

Bradley had to admit that he did admire Annabelle. She was an excellent businesswoman and she'd survived a great deal in her personal life. *Is surviving,* he corrected himself, recalling her nightmare. The image of her dressed in floppy slippers, flannel pajamas and a well-worn heavy terry-cloth robe with her hair in disarray and her dark brown eyes exposing a vulnerability that shook him filled his mind. It was not a seductive image, but it stirred something deep within him. Again the urge to help her get over her fear of men taunted him. But she wasn't what he wanted in a wife, and she deserved a man who would stay with her.

Annabelle will make some house-husband very happy one day, he told himself a little later after bidding his sister goodbye and hanging up. And he'd be happy for her, he added.

Chapter Eight

Annabelle slept restlessly. At three in the morning she found herself awake. After tossing and turning for twenty minutes in an attempt to go back to sleep, she finally gave up and got out of bed. At four o'clock she was sitting at her kitchen table, drinking coffee and making lists.

"Invitations are unnecessary since we're calling everyone," she murmured. Then, remembering that this marriage had to be as public as possible, she added, "But I'll have to send a written notice to the newspaper."

She felt fairly confident that the flowers could be ordered without any problem. The food, however, might prove to be more difficult to arrange. Finding a private room at one of the better restaurants, or any restaurant for that matter, on such short notice could be impossible. Of course, there were always caterers, she reminded herself. Quickly she counted the number of guests. Only family was invited. That would make things easier. Including the triplets, the number came to fourteen.

"And," she said, giving in to a need to walk off some of her nervous tension by rising and wandering into the living room, "we'll have the ceremony right here. It'll be easier with the babies." Besides, considering all the stories she'd heard about people having to book churches and chapels a year in advance, she guessed that having it in her own living room would be a necessity.

"I just hope the Reverend Brown is free," she said anxiously, sinking into a chair and cradling her coffee cup in her hands.

By ten that morning, she'd gotten all the information about acquiring the marriage license. She'd also determined that the reverend could sandwich her and Bradley's ceremony in between two others. "Luckily you live near the church," he'd said as they decided on eleven o'clock on the designated Saturday. Adding to her nervousness, he also insisted on meeting with her and Bradley before the day of the wedding. She'd been a member of his congregation for several years but wasn't as active in the church as Linda, so he didn't know her well enough to be aware that she and Bradley had just met, and she didn't offer that information. She was fairly certain he would counsel them to wait a while until they'd had time to get to know one another better. He might even refuse to perform the wedding. She made a note to warn Bradley not to mention the length of their association.

Planning the wedding was a great deal more complicated than she had imagined, she thought as she hung up after promising to get back to the reverend. "But I can work out a schedule so that Bradley and I can do everything that's required," she assured herself firmly. "I've arranged week-long business meetings for fifty to a hundred people on two days' notice. I can do this."

Next she called one of the better restaurants in town to make reservations for the rehearsal dinner. They didn't have any private rooms available, but they could put everyone at a single table in a far corner of a smaller dining room. "So far, so good," she said, checking that off her list.

Then she began calling caterers to provide the food for after the wedding. "Business meetings are easier to plan," she grumbled a little while later. She'd just finished calling the third catering service on her list and been informed that they were booked so solid she could have been the First Lady and they'd have had to turn her down.

By the time Bradley called at noon, she was ready to scream. Not a single caterer was available.

"Offer them more money," he suggested.

She scowled into the receiver. His remark made her sound like a novice at dealing with business people. "I already tried that."

He heard the frustration in her voice and felt a rush of sympathy for her. "I'm sure you'll think of something," he replied soothingly.

"Thanks." She knew he was trying to be encouraging, but at this moment that didn't help. Before she could stop herself, she heard herself adding dryly, "What I'd like to know is how I got elected to be the one to stay here and have all this fun."

It had never occurred to Bradley that planning a simple wedding could rattle the very efficient Ms. Royd. "You're the bride. The bride always plans the wedding."

From the tone of his voice, she could visualize him frowning impatiently. The image raised her ire. "How chauvinistic of you."

"I'm sorry," he apologized gruffly. "I'd be there to help if I could, but as I explained to you, I contracted for this job months ago." Curiously he actually found himself wishing he could fly back that minute and help her. *I just don't want anything to go wrong,* he told himself.

Annabelle scowled at herself. She was the one without a job, and her career prospects could look dim if Bradley hadn't been willing to go through with this marriage. Not to mention the possibility of a badly tarnished reputation, she added. Of course, *his* reputation, as well as his business, was on the line, too. "I guess we're having our first fight," she said with an edge of self-consciousness.

"Someone once told me that the first great hurdle of any marriage was surviving the planning of the wedding," he replied, relieved by the offer of peace in her tone. Amusement entered his voice. "I think the person who told me that had just broken his second engagement. In the next breath he swore he was going to become a confirmed bachelor or elope with his next fiancée."

Annabelle smiled wryly. "I can understand that."

Bradley's tone again became serious. "Just remember that this wedding has to happen. I don't care if we have to eat hot dogs and popcorn at the reception."

"That would be something to tell the grandchildren," Annabelle tossed back, then gasped. She'd said that as if this marriage was the real thing. "If there were going to be grandchildren, which there aren't," she added quickly, wanting to assure him that she intended to abide by the conditions they'd set for the marriage.

Bradley had this sudden vision of a little boy who looked like him and a little girl who looked like Annabelle. But they weren't in children's clothing and playing with toys. Instead they were wearing little tailored suits and carrying briefcases. Immediately he pushed the images from his mind.

"You'll have to come back to Pittsburgh early next week for a day," Annabelle continued, her manner businesslike. "We have to apply for the license. We also have to have blood tests and physicals. I'll set up appointments with my doctor. He'll have the forms required by the license bureau. And we have to meet with the Reverend Brown."

"Fine," Bradley replied in the same clipped tone. This was a business deal, he reminded himself curtly. There was nothing personal between them, and children most definitely did not fit into the picture, he added sternly, still shocked by the images that had come into his mind. "I'll be back on Monday." He gave Annabelle his hotel phone number and his room number. He also gave her the phone number of the company where he was working, in case of an emergency. Then he hung up.

"He's right," she said as she dialed the reverend's number to set up an appointment with him. "It doesn't matter how the wedding happens, as long as it happens." She grimaced to herself. "And no more cracks about grandchildren," she ordered.

To her relief the afternoon went more smoothly. She found a florist who could provide the flowers. Linda went with her to help choose the colors and the kinds. And when the florist mentioned that he had an arched trellis that would fit nicely into the living room and provide a backdrop for the ceremony, Annabelle agreed. After all, Bradley had left her in charge, and he did say he wanted the wedding to look authentic.

Later that night, Linda solved the problem of the caterer. "Frank's sister is studying home economics at the university. She and some of her friends will come and fix a brunch," she offered. "All we have to do is add some bread rolls, Danishes and a few other goodies to your order when you arrange for the wedding cake."

"The wedding cake!" Annabelle grabbed her notepad. "I completely forgot about the cake."

"And the champagne?" Linda questioned.

"And the champagne," Annabelle admitted.

"Maybe I'd better go over that list with you," Linda suggested.

Annabelle agreed. Planning a business meeting was definitely a lot less complicated, she decided.

* * *

By Monday, Annabelle was certain she had the situation well in hand. She felt she was again in control of her life as she waited at the airport for Bradley to disembark. But when she saw him coming toward her, a warmth began down deep in her abdomen and spread through her. His eyes had dark circles under them, as if he hadn't been sleeping well, and his expression was grim. Still, to her he looked even more handsome than she remembered. But what truly disconcerted her was the urge to wrap her arms around him and attempt to ease the grimness from his face. *He's looking like that because of our impending marriage,* she reminded herself. *The last person he honestly wants greeting him is me.* The thought hurt. *You're not supposed to feel anything,* she scolded herself. *The two of you are getting married, but it isn't personal.*

Bradley saw her. She was wearing a pair of slacks and a bulky sweater. Her hair was hanging loose, giving a softness to her features. When she was dressed like that he could easily believe she was the wife he wanted. But this was not the real Annabelle Royd, he told himself. At least, not the total woman. It was, however, he thought grudgingly, the image that had been haunting his dreams.

"You look very nice today," he said as he reached her. He could not keep the edge of accusation out of his voice. "Looks as if I'm going to be taking a lot of cold showers."

Startled, Annabelle studied him. So he wasn't as immune to her as she'd thought. The old fear stirred inside, but it was overshadowed by a surge of pleasure.

Damn! Bradley cursed himself. He didn't want to frighten her out of this wedding. But when his gaze narrowed on her face, searching for signs of flight, they weren't there. Were her fears diminishing? he wondered. If so, the next two years might not be difficult, after all. Then he scowled at himself. Thoughts like that will only lead to complications, he warned himself. Besides she probably wasn't showing any fear because she trusted him not to make any advances.

"Guess we have a busy schedule today," he said, ordering himself to put any thoughts of an intimate relationship out of his mind. "I've got an eight-o'clock flight out this evening. I should have the preliminary work on this current job done by Friday. I wish I could take some time off and we could go somewhere to make it look as if we were going on a honeymoon, but I can't. So I figured you can fly back to Kansas City with me on Sunday and help me with the final investigation and the report." He gave a shrug. "Or you can spend your time sight-seeing. It just wouldn't look right if I went back without my new bride."

Annabelle had the feeling that he would have preferred to leave her in Pittsburgh for the duration of their marriage, and that realization stung. He might not be as immune to her as he professed, but he obviously wanted to keep his distance. "I'll help with the investigation," she replied, leading the way to the car. She'd never been very interested in sight-seeing. Besides, she wasn't used to not working. And he had said he planned to train her as his assistant. The sooner she had something other than thoughts of him to occupy her mind, the better.

Bradley's eyes caught the gentle swing of her hips as she moved. He was going to be taking a lot of cold showers.

The license bureau was their first stop. By the time they finished there, they had to rush to make their appointment with the minister.

Annabelle fought a wave of discomfort as the elderly clergyman spoke about the responsibilities of marriage and the sacredness of it. "But I can't imagine Annabelle entering into anything she hasn't thought out thoroughly," he finished with a smile.

"You have my word that I'll take good care of her," Bradley assured him.

There was a promise in his voice that ignited a warmth in Annabelle. Then she chastised herself. He'd meant what he'd said, but not in the way a man who was in love with a woman meant it. A twinge of regret shook her. *You barely know Bradley. You can't really be feeling anything other than a surface attraction to him and that won't last.*

"I'm very pleased to hear you say that," the Reverend Brown was saying to Bradley with a fatherly smile. Then dividing his attention between Bradley and Annabelle, he asked, "Do you have your own vows you would like to use or shall we go with the traditional?"

"The traditional is fine with me," Annabelle replied. When Bradley hesitated, she glanced at him. She couldn't believe he would consider writing their vows.

It suddenly occurred to her that he'd decided he couldn't go through with this farce of a marriage. The thought caused a wave of anxiety. *I can handle whatever happens,* she assured herself. She'd survived a great deal more than the injury Randall Swynite's accusation could cause her.

"The traditional vows are fine with me," Bradley said after a moment. A smile played at one corner of his mouth. "However, if the bride is still supposed to vow to love, honor and *obey,* I'd suggest we change or omit the *obey.* Annie is a woman with a mind of her own. Maybe you should make it 'listen to my husband once in a while'?"

The Reverend Brown grinned. "I usually say 'cherish' now."

Annabelle forced herself to join in the men's good-natured laughter. After all, it had been merely a jest. At least on the surface. She was getting to know a few of Bradley's little quirks. One was a slight twitch of his jaw when he was making a joke to cover something that irritated or annoyed him, and she'd noticed that twitch when he'd made the suggestion about removing "obey" from the ceremony. She told herself to ignore it. But his implication that she could prove difficult to get along with was still needling her when they left the church.

"I suppose," she said, "you'd prefer a wife who bowed to your every whim, hung on your every word, agreed to your every opinion, waited on you—" her expression became mischievous "—as if you were a knight in a castle, Sir Perceval."

He rewarded her reference to his name with a raised eyebrow, as if to say he thought she'd gone a bit too far. "I want a wife who would be satisfied with staying at home and raising our children."

For one brief moment Annabelle found herself wanting to fit that picture. But she knew she wouldn't be happy. "Then I wish you luck with your second wife," she replied. "I don't like housework. I hire my sister to do mine once a week. It works out well for both of us."

"And you think children should be raised by nannies," he finished for her, glad all this was coming out into the open. Hearing her admit to exactly how she felt about being a housewife and mother would help him keep things in perspective.

"No." They had reached the car, and she turned to face him. "If I have any children, I want to be their primary caretaker. But that doesn't mean I have to give up my career. I should be able to find some sort of job I could do from my home. With today's technology, I can have easy access to a central office complex, or I can do independent consulting."

"A crib in the corner and you at your desk with a computer and modem and you're set, right?" Bradley said dryly.

She met his gaze coolly. "Something like that."

Sliding in behind the wheel, Bradley envisioned Annabelle in her business suit, sitting in her living room at a desk just as he'd described. The two children he'd pictured earlier were in a crib in the corner playing with their own little computers. What surprised him was that he didn't find this scene as distasteful as he'd expected to. But that wasn't the kind of scene he wanted played out in his home.

"We have time for a quick lunch before your doctor's appointment," Annabelle said, changing the subject. Bradley had the image of the woman he wanted for his wife well formed in his mind and she didn't fit it. But then she'd known that all along. And he was welcome to his sweet little housewife, she assured herself. All she wanted was to get this wedding over with, survive the marriage, and then get on with her life.

Two hours later, they were leaving the doctor's office. "That takes care of everything, unless you want to have a double-ring ceremony," Annabelle said as they again climbed into her car. "In that case we need to stop by a jeweler's so you can pick out a ring and have it sized. Otherwise, I can go by and get one for myself on my own."

"My wearing a ring would make our marriage look more authentic," he replied.

Annabelle nodded in agreement and drove to a nearby jewelry store, where they picked out matching bands.

"Lady Luck must be smiling down on you," the jeweler said with a smile. "We have your sizes." His smile broadened. "Since they don't have to be sized, I can guarantee we can have them engraved by Friday if you wish."

Bradley looked questioningly at the man. "Engraved?"

"A lot of couples have their names and the date of their wedding engraved on the inside of the band." He winked conspiratorially. "That way if you should forget your wedding date, you only have to slip the ring off and look inside. It saves you the embarrassment of forgetting your anniversary. I've had husbands swear it's saved their marriage."

Bradley shrugged. "I'm a firm believer in tradition."

Annabelle's jaw tensed. Again he was making it clear that when he married for real he wanted a traditional marriage and a traditional wife. She smiled coolly at Bradley to let him know she'd gotten his message yet again and was getting bored by it. Then, turning back toward the jeweler, she said, "Yes, I think having them engraved would be a fine idea."

"How should they read?" the man asked, his pen poised above the order form.

"Annie and Bradley," Bradley replied, spelling the names, then adding the date of the wedding.

A sudden urge came over Annabelle. She told herself to forget it, but it refused to go away. After all, he felt free to make his preferences known, she reasoned. Turnabout was fair play. Smiling what she hoped was a beguiling smile, she said, "I'd really rather it read Annie and Perceval."

Bradley turned and scowled at her. The jeweler looked confused.

Maybe she had gone too far, Annabelle admitted, but there was no turning back now. She lowered her voice and leaned closer to the shopkeeper. "My fiancé's first initial stands for Perceval, but he doesn't like anyone to know." She smiled. "I've always wanted to marry a knight in shining armor."

The man grinned back, then looked inquiringly at Bradley.

Touché, Bradley thought. He realized he'd been very adamant about letting her know what he wanted in a wife. It was only fair that she let him know she had thoughts about what *she* wanted in a husband. "If it's Perceval she wants, then it's Perceval she shall have," he replied, taking a step back and performing a deep bow as if he were a knight of old addressing his lady.

The jeweler laughed. "I like to see a couple who can deal with each other's little quirks with a sense of humor," he said as he quickly changed the name on the order form. His expression becoming fatherly, he turned his attention to Annabelle and Bradley. "I'd say you two have a good life in front of you. I wish you all the best."

Annabelle forced a smile. Yes, she hoped that she and Bradley would indeed have good lives ahead of them. But those lives weren't going to be with each other. Except for the next two years, she corrected. A small wave of nervousness shook her. She brushed it aside. The two years would be a cinch. The challenge was getting through the next few days.

Chapter Nine

Annabelle stood looking at herself in her mirror. It was Saturday, and in a few minutes the minister's teenage son was going to be playing the wedding march on his electric guitar. When Linda had suggested that he perform at her wedding, at first Annabelle had balked. Actually, the suggestion had been made out of desperation. The teenager was the only musician available. "It's either him or a record," Linda had said. Given that choice, Annabelle had decided that it couldn't hurt to have the boy audition. And she'd been glad she had. She admitted that the sound was a bit unusual, but she found she liked the twang the guitar added to the melody. She grinned. And the triplets loved it.

She drew a deep breath. Even the rehearsal and the rehearsal dinner had gone well. Bradley's family had proved to be very pleasant. His sister had called her a

few days earlier to offer her help with the wedding.
But with Helen living in California, they both knew
this was only a pretext. Luckily, Annabelle had only
had to field a few questions before she could honestly
say she had to be going or she would be late for an appointment. Helen had attempted, however, at the rehearsal and the dinner that followed, to corner
Annabelle a couple of times to ask questions about
how she and Bradley had met. But Bradley had come
to Annabelle's rescue.

Her own parents had accepted Bradley well. Like
Linda, they'd expressed surprise at the suddenness of
the wedding, but they hadn't tried to talk her out of it.

"Linda says you know what you're doing. You've
always been levelheaded. I've never had to worry
about any decisions you've made before," her father
had said to her. "So your mother and I won't question this one. We'll just assume you've thought it out
and you are certain this is what you want. We wish you
and Bradley the very best."

Annabelle had no idea what Bradley's parents had
said to him privately, but they were kind to her and, on
the surface at least, appeared to be accepting the marriage.

"So far, so good," she said to her image in the mirror, then rapped her fist lightly on her dresser as she
added, "Knock on wood." She told herself she wasn't
superstitious, but this was not a time she wanted to
take chances with fate.

She'd tried to keep the wedding as simple as possible. And she felt she'd succeeded. Linda was her ma-
tron of honor, and Bradley's father was standing up

for him as best man. There were to be no other atten-
dants. Annabelle had also decided that the men should
wear suits instead of tuxedos. This saved her the trouble of having to get their sizes, rent the garments and
then arrange for their return. Besides, this less formal
attire was more in keeping with the small, intimate
ceremony.

As for Linda, it was March and the spring fashions
were in the stores. They'd found her a cute, pastel-
colored suit with a floral design. Annabelle had been
planning to wear a simple but stylish suit herself.
However, nothing she tried on satisfied her.

On a whim, she and Linda had stopped by a bridal
shop. She hadn't been able to resist trying on one of
the gowns. It had been such fun, like playing dress-up
as a child. Once she got started, she'd tried on several. In the end, she bought one. It was cream-colored
instead of pure white, but it was all lace and satin, and
in it she felt like a real bride.

A knock sounded on her door. Immediately it was
followed by Linda's entrance. "They're ready. Dad's
waiting at the foot of the stairs," she said, nervousness bringing a slight flush to her cheeks. Quickly she
arranged Annabelle's veil, then stepped back. "You
look lovely," she declared, tears beginning to brim in
her eyes. "I'd give you a final hug, but I don't want to
muss anything."

"You won't muss anything," Annabelle assured
her, inviting the hug. Linda had been a brick
throughout this whole thing. She'd even found a photographer. He was another college student, a friend of
Frank's sister, who was majoring in journalism. An-

nabelle hadn't even thought of hiring a photographer. And she was very grateful to Linda for adding it to the list. An omission like that could have looked highly suspicious to anyone trying to find proof that this wedding wasn't the real thing.

Linda hugged her sister tightly, then stepped back and again arranged the veil. A loud guitar chord sounded from downstairs, signaling them that it was time for the ceremony to begin.

Annabelle took a fortifying breath.

"Bradley looks great," Linda said in a whisper as they left the bedroom.

Bradley *always* looks great, Annabelle thought. Again, a notion that had been trying to gain substance for the past few days pushed itself forward. She scowled. He's made it very clear that he wants to keep a distance between us, she reminded herself, shoving the notion back into the shadows.

Just concentrate on getting through this ceremony, she ordered herself as she greeted her father with a hug.

"You look lovely," he said, pride glistening in his eyes.

For one brief second Annabelle found herself wishing Bradley would think she looked lovely, too. *Don't be foolish,* she chided herself. "I love you," she whispered to her father, returning his hug. Then, taking a final deep breath to calm a sudden spasm of nerves, she stood quietly beside him a few feet from the entrance to the living room as Linda preceded them inside.

Suddenly the strains of the bridal chorus began. It was time. As she entered the room on her father's arm, she saw the surprise on Bradley's face. Obviously he hadn't expected her to wear a formal gown. But then, she reminded herself, she hadn't planned on wearing one, either. When his surprise turned to an expression of masculine appreciation, a rush of pleasure swept through her. *Now don't let yourself start thinking that look means anything,* she cautioned sharply as the notion that had been nagging at her during the past few days again surfaced. *He's only pleased because I'm dressed like a traditional bride. I'm sure that, in his mind, it makes this ceremony appear more valid.* As if to prove her point, Bradley's mouth tilted into a crooked smile, and he got that cool gleam in his eyes she'd seen when he was especially happy with the way a business deal was going. The pleasure she'd felt faded.

Finally the vows were said and Bradley was lifting the veil. Then he was taking her in his arms. The kiss began lightly. She thought she was prepared for it, but her first reaction was a desire to recoil. Then the warmth of his lips began to take over her senses. They enticed her like nothing she'd ever experienced before. The sensation was subtle yet exciting, and she didn't want it to end. Not even thinking about what she was doing, she wound her arms around his neck.

All during the ceremony, Bradley had been trying to concentrate on the minister, the flowers, anything but the woman beside him. But his mind had kept coming back to the kiss that would end the wedding. He knew he shouldn't be interested in what it would feel like to hold Annabelle in his arms. That wasn't part of their deal. It was just male curiosity that made him wonder what kissing her firmly would be like, he assured himself. He recalled that the one time he'd kissed her lightly, her lips had been softer than he'd expected, and she'd seemed to taste mildly sweet. Then he'd frowned at himself for even remembering that. As he'd lifted the veil from her face, he'd cautioned himself to keep this kiss cool. He didn't want her suddenly getting frightened and bolting out of the room. Or even more importantly, he added, he didn't want her attacking him with another martial-arts blow.

When their lips met, he was surprised to discover that hers seemed even softer than he'd remembered and the sweetness was still there. He found himself wanting a longer, fuller taste. Keep it short, he warned himself, then he realized that her arms were beginning to entwine around his neck. So she was willing to allow a traditional kiss to go with the traditional gown, he mused. That suited him just fine. *It's only playacting, but it will satisfy my curiosity once and for all,* he told himself, as his hold tightened on her and he deepened the kiss.

Her body molded against his and he was acutely aware of the firmness of her curves. Desire sparked within him. Almost immediately it threatened to become a raging fire. Startled by the strength of his reaction to a simple, public kiss, he quickly lifted his head away from hers.

Annabelle had been lost in a whirlpool of sensations. When his mouth had claimed hers more fully, she'd experienced a rush of pleasure so intense her toes had curled. Next came a heat that began deep in her abdomen and spread through her like a raging fire. Then there had been the awakening of something that felt like a hunger...a need...a craving. She wasn't certain which exactly. Whatever it was, it was strong. Suddenly the contact was broken. A feeling of foolishness spread through her. Then she saw it—the desire in Bradley's eyes. It was just a glimpse before they became cool with control. But it had been there, and the notion that had been taunting her returned. No time to think about it now, though, she told herself, as the jabbering of one of the triplets reminded her that there was a roomful of people watching.

She flushed, wondering if the kiss had embarrassed their audience. But when she turned, all she saw were smiling faces. Obviously, the kiss had looked perfectly acceptable for the final seal of the ceremony.

For the next few hours, Annabelle was kept busy visiting with their guests. But finally the brunch was over. The girls who had prepared it had now cleaned up, stored all of the leftovers and gone. The members of Bradley's family had left to return to their hotel, and her parents had gone next door with Linda and Frank and the triplets. She and Bradley were alone.

Sinking onto the couch, Annabelle picked up her bouquet. It was pink roses in a cloud of baby's breath. She thought it was the prettiest bouquet she'd ever seen. The corsage the florist had worked into the center was gone. Linda had taken it. She had a friend who knew how to dry flowers and was going to dry the corsage for Annabelle as a memento of the wedding.

But even without the corsage, the bouquet was beautiful.

Annabelle kicked off her shoes, then lifted her tired feet and let them come to rest, crossed at the ankles, on the coffee table. A wistful smile played across her face as she tossed the bouquet into the air, then caught it.

"Nice catch," Bradley said, removing his jacket.

"I decided it was appropriate," she replied. "I didn't throw my bouquet at the wedding because other than Linda's toddlers and your five-year-old niece, there were no unmarried female guests. I'm the closest to being in that category, and since I have hopes of having a husband and family some day, I seemed like the most logical choice to catch my bouquet." There were two comfortable, upholstered chairs flanking the couch. Bradley had also removed his tie, and now he flung both jacket and tie over the back of one and sat down in the other. Then he undid the top couple of buttons of his shirt. She'd been watching him as she spoke and the warm curling sensation had again begun deep in her abdomen.

Suddenly worried that he might think she had plans of trapping him in this marriage, she leaned down, lifted her skirt enough to find the lacy garter the woman at the bridal store had given her and slipped it off. "Here," she said, tossing it to him. "We didn't throw this, either, since there were no unattached males anywhere near marriageable age in attendance. You can toss it to yourself for luck. Hopefully next time we each walk down the aisle, it will be with someone we plan to spend a lifetime with."

"Yeah," Bradley replied, catching the garter. But instead of immediately tossing it into the air and catching it once again, he studied the blue-satin and white-lace concoction. He didn't understand why, but it irked him that Annabelle Royd—Annabelle Franklin, he corrected himself—was already thinking of a new husband. *I'm just tired,* he decided, and tossed the garter into the air, then caught it. "Good luck to both of us," he said.

Annabelle tensed. Now was as good a time as any to act on the notion that had been tormenting her for the past few days. But when she started to speak, a wave of nervousness swept over her. What if he refused? And there was a big likelihood that he would. It would be embarrassing, but she could live with it, she decided. Then she reminded herself of the kiss and the desire she'd seen in his eyes. After all, he was a man, and two years was a long time, she reasoned, attempting to bolster her courage. *Go on,* she ordered herself. *Ask him.* "I have a favor I'd like to ask," she said stiffly. Her throat suddenly constricted and nothing more would come out.

"What is it?" Bradley prodded when she didn't continue. Her sudden nervousness caused him to wonder if, after the kiss at the altar, she was going to ask to have a padlock put on her bedroom door. Well, he hadn't been the one to initiate so full a contact. He'd planned to keep it reasonably simple and uninvolved.

Annabelle wet her dry lips, then continued evenly, "I do want to have a husband and family one day. But I seem to have a small problem."

Again recalling the blow he'd taken in the chest, Bradley thought he wouldn't classify her problem as small. "The nightmares," he said.

Annabelle nodded. "I thought I'd gotten over my fears. I even dated a little. But the relationships were always platonic. I never felt any real physical attraction toward the men I went out with." Again a wave of nervousness swept over her. This part could get humiliating. Again she recalled the desire she'd seen in his eyes, and it gave her courage.

"Anyway, I have to admit that while I know I'm not what you want in a wife and you are not what I want in a husband . . ." She glanced away momentarily, unable to look at him. This last declaration wasn't exactly true. He had a lot of the qualities she wanted. He was honest, intelligent and had a sense of humor. But he wasn't in love with her, and that was the most important requirement for her husband. She wanted a man who loved her as much as Frank loved Linda. Her gaze shifted back to him. "I do find you physically attractive."

Bradley liked this admission more than he cared to admit.

Annabelle saw the spark of interest in his eyes. It helped her go on. "The truth is, it's this attraction that has forced me to realize I have a lingering fear of intimacy," she confessed. Her stomach knotted as she once again recalled the rape. "The attack was painful, and now I'm afraid that any intimacy will be just as painful. I sustained no lasting physical injury during the incident, and everything I've read has assured me that I should be able to have a pleasurable, intimate relationship with a man. But I feel that until I actually have the experience, I'm going to continue to fear it.''

Bradley was fairly certain he knew now what she was going to ask. A part of him warned that this could only lead to trouble, but another part of him was too interested to stop her. "I suppose it's only natural to fear something that gave you pain," he said.

She saw the interest in his eyes and knew that he knew where this was leading. And he wasn't stopping her. *I could be setting myself up for some real humiliation,* she cautioned. What if she invited the man into her bed, then bolted like a frightened rabbit? Her jaw tensed. If he agrees, I'll go through with it, she promised herself. "Anyway," she continued, "I've been thinking that as long as we're going to be living together for a while... I was wondering if you might consider helping me get over this fear.''

"I know from experience that you can be a very dangerous woman, Annie," he said.

Annabelle stiffened. He was going to refuse her.

But Bradley decided it was stupid to continue to try to deny the attraction he felt toward her. In fact, this could be a good thing. What he felt was only physical. Once he'd shared her bed for a while, the allure should fade and eventually go away. By the time their marriage ended she would be completely out of his system. "Two years can be a long time," he said. "Having an intimate relationship could help us both get through this a little easier.''

He agreed. Annabelle gave a sigh of relief. "You don't have to worry about an unwanted pregnancy, either," she assured him quickly. "I've taken precautions."

"That's good," he replied, thinking how nice it was to deal with such a practical woman. "We wouldn't want any complications when we're ready to end this marriage."

"No, we don't want any complications," she agreed. Suddenly she felt uncertain. What if he was a rough lover, or what if he wanted to attempt intimacy immediately? She wasn't sure she was ready yet. She shifted her gaze to the bouquet. *I can handle whatever happens,* she told herself, focusing her attention on a perfect pink rosebud.

Bradley studied her. She looked indecisive and a little scared. Again he experienced a strong desire to protect her. "There's no need to rush into this," he said. "We can take a while for you to get used to having me around."

Annabelle drew a calming breath.

Watching the slight lift of her breasts, Bradley felt the embers of desire again ignite. Grudgingly he admitted that no other woman had ever been able to arouse him so easily. It was the challenge, he decided. He'd always liked challenges. Suddenly the house seemed small and confining. "Why don't you change into something a little less bulky," he suggested, "and we'll go out to dinner."

She told herself she was being silly. Bradley's behavior gave no evidence of his having an unquenchable, driving passion for her. In fact, quite the opposite. Hadn't he, only a moment ago, made it clear he was in no rush to act on her request? However, the thought of having other people around for a while brought a sense of relief. "Sounds like a great idea," she agreed quickly.

Escaping to her room, she had barely closed the door when it occurred to her that she would need help unfastening the wedding gown. Asking Bradley for assistance was the reasonable thing to do. But her fear resurfaced and she balked at this idea. After laying aside her veil, she tried to work the buttons and zipper loose on her own, but finally had to admit defeat. For a second she was tempted to call Linda and ask her to come over and help. "You are being ridiculous," she admonished herself, imagining the shock on Linda's face if she made such a request.

Going back downstairs, she found Bradley sitting where she'd left him, toying with the garter, frowning. Maybe he already regretted having agreed to help her overcome her fear of intimacy, she thought. If that was true, she wished he would say so.

But instead, he simply looked surprised to see her.

"I can't unfasten this dress by myself," she said self-consciously.

Bradley rose and moved toward her. She looked so damn kissable, he thought. He'd been sitting there thinking about how she would feel when he did finally take her in his arms. Just the remembered softness of her lips had caused his blood to flow faster. This was going to take control, he'd been telling himself. Now there she was asking him to help her out of her dress. "Turn around," he ordered gruffly as he reached her.

His attitude irked Annabelle. He acted as if she'd asked him to go out and slay a dragon. "I'm sorry to be such an inconvenience."

"You're not an inconvenience," he replied, trying to concentrate on the buttons and not the smooth, silky texture of her back. "You're a temptation," he added honestly.

Annabelle's anger immediately vanished. Unable to stop herself, she grinned. Not only was he still interested in helping her over her fear, he wasn't at all immune to her. *And I'm definitely not immune to him,* she added, as his fingers, brushing her skin, sent currents of excitement shooting through her. The fear she'd expected to feel with his first contact wasn't there.

Bradley finished with the buttons and lowered the zipper. As the dress fell loose from her shoulders, the creaminess of her skin taunted him even more. One friendly little kiss to create an air of romance can't hurt, he decided. Leaning down, he gently brushed her shoulder with his mouth.

The touch of his lips was like a hot brand scorching her skin. Annabelle stiffened, startled by the intensity of her body's response to this featherlight contact.

Immediately Bradley stepped back. "I didn't mean to frighten you," he said in gruff apology. "Just thought I would try a small taste."

Her heart was racing. "It didn't frighten me," she confessed, keeping her back toward him, not wanting him to see how shaken this simple action on his part had left her.

Bradley noted that her breathing was slightly irregular. If it wasn't from fear, then maybe he wouldn't have to go quite as slowly as he'd thought....

"Actually it felt rather good," Annabelle added, wishing he'd do it again.

He heard the invitation in her voice. For her sake, he still planned to move slowly, but another little kiss couldn't hurt. Stepping forward, he wound his arms around her lightly and kissed the other shoulder.

"That felt even better," Annabelle said shakily. Not to mention the exquisite delight of his embrace, she added to herself.

Bradley kissed the nape of her neck. She tasted intoxicating. With one hand he gently cupped her breast.

Even through the fabric of her dress, Annabelle felt the heat of his touch. She leaned against him, her body searching for a firmer contact. *You're moving too fast,* a part of her screamed while another part cried that she couldn't move fast enough. "I really should go upstairs and get out of this dress," she said.

Let her go, Bradley ordered himself. His arms aching from the effort, he let his hands travel slowly over her midriff as he stepped back, then fully relinquished his hold.

A sense of desertion swept through her. She ordered her legs and feet to start walking, but still she hesitated. She didn't want to lose this rush of sensation.

Bradley saw her hesitation. *You're pushing it, old boy,* he warned himself. But he couldn't forget the way she'd seemed to burst into flame beneath his touch.

"Maybe I should come upstairs with you, just in case you need further assistance," he suggested.

"Maybe you should," Annabelle replied, then couldn't believe she was encouraging him.

But as she climbed the stairs with him behind her, she had no desire to call a halt.

She reached the landing, then continued into her room. Acutely aware of Bradley behind her, she turned and glanced back when the sound of his footsteps suddenly stopped. He was standing in the doorway of her room, regarding her with a stern expression.

"Are you sure you want me to come in?" he asked. Without question, he wanted to follow her, but she'd been through one trauma. He wasn't going to provide her with another.

Looking at him, a need so strong it was like a physical force came over her. "Yes, I want you to come in," she replied.

Cautiously he entered. "Any time you get scared and want to stop, tell me," he ordered.

She nodded, then began removing the dress.

Bradley approached and helped. Hoping to maintain a slow pace, he touched her as little as possible. When she stepped out of the dress, he backed away, giving her room to pick it up.

Feeling a sudden acute wave of nervousness, Annabelle bought some time by carrying the dress to the closet and hanging it up carefully. She could feel Bradley watching her, and a flush reddened her cheeks as she caught a glimpse in the mirror of herself dressed only in the lacy bra, half slip and panty hose. Then she met Bradley's gaze. The color of his eyes had darkened, and there was a heat in them that added fuel to the embers smoldering within her. Her embarrassment was forgotten and she heard herself saying, "One of us is overdressed."

He smiled. "Guess I should take care of that."

As he began unbuttoning his shirt, Annabelle moved toward him. She had expected to feel like running from the room. Instead, she was being drawn to him like a moth to a flame. "I'll help," she volunteered as she reached him.

Bradley noticed that her fingers were trembling slightly as she worked the buttons open. Go slow, he ordered himself, and be prepared to stop. But that would not be easy. His gaze fell on the exposed moon-shaped crescents of her breasts above the confines of the lacy bra. Their soft rise and fall seemed to beckon for his attention.

Sliding off his shirt, Annabelle was enthralled by the sight that greeted her. She tossed the garment aside, then slowly ran her hands over the sturdy musculature of his shoulders and chest. "You have a very nice body," she said with husky admiration.

"Yours shows great promise of being even nicer," he replied, slipping his hands around her and working loose the fastenings of her bra.

The way he touched her as he took his time undressing her fueled the embers he had sparked until it was as if a raging fire were burning within her.

Bradley could feel her body's response beneath his hands and see it in her eyes. Proceeding at a pace that he hoped would not frighten her grew more difficult by the moment. Leaving her, he walked to the bed and tossed the covers aside. Then he glanced toward her questioningly, allowing her to decide if she wanted to continue.

Chewing nervously on her bottom lip, Annabelle approached the bed. The time was growing closer for her to face her fear. Her heart began pounding so hard it felt as if it was trying to break out of her chest. But she didn't want to stop this now. "You're still over-dressed," she heard herself saying, and marveled at her ability to put a sentence together.

Bradley grinned. "Not for long." As she climbed onto the bed, he quickly discarded the remainder of his clothing.

Joining her, he sensed her sudden uneasiness. Don't rush this, he ordered himself. Until this moment he hadn't realized how important it had become to him that he do this right, that he make this an enjoyable experience for her. It's my ego, he reasoned. Then brushing aside all thoughts but those of giving plea-sure, he concentrated on her. Her body had tensed and he read the fear in her eyes. "I'm not going to rush you," he promised gruffly.

Annabelle felt her muscles relaxing as his lips trailed light kisses over her and his hands massaged and ca-ressed her. Once again she became lost in a sea of en-ticing sensations.

Bradley was certain her body was ready to accept him. But he didn't want to surprise her and bring back her fear. "I think the time has come to move to the next stage," he murmured huskily, nibbling on her earlobe.

"I think you're right," she agreed, her breathing ragged. "If we wait any longer, I think I might spontaneously ignite." A sudden vision caused her to giggle. "They'd write about you and me in the tabloids. I can see the heading now—HUSBAND'S LOVEMAKING SO PASSIONATE, WIFE GOES UP IN FLAMES ON WEDDING NIGHT. You'll be a legend in your own time." She grimaced quirkily. "Or have they already printed a story like that?"

Bradley laughed gently. "Probably," he conceded. Annabelle had proved to be a great deal more fun than he'd ever thought she could be. *And I want to keep it that way,* he added, forcing his movements to remain slow and concentrating on her every reaction.

He felt her tense when he claimed her, then she breathed a sigh of relief and smiled. "Either you're very good at this or there wasn't anything for me to fear in the first place," she said, her hands trailing over his chest, luxuriating in the solid feel of him.

"My ego would like to believe it was me, but that'd probably be a lie," he replied, thinking that no woman had ever felt this good to him.

Annabelle gasped with delight as he began to carry her to even greater heights of ecstasy. "As long as you keep doing what you're doing, you can believe anything you like," she said. Then all thoughts of talking vanished, as her mind and body were consumed in a torrent of wonderful, raging sensation.

Chapter Ten

Annabelle stared out the window of the airplane. There was regret in her expression. It was Sunday evening, and she and Bradley were flying to Kansas City to finish the job he'd been working on there. Other than the few minutes she'd spent going over to Linda's to make final arrangements for her sister to take care of her house while she was away, this was the first time either Annabelle or Bradley had left her home since the wedding. A smile curled her lips. Luckily there had been plenty of leftovers from the brunch to keep them sustained.

Annabelle's smile deepened as she recalled Linda's commenting on how relaxed and happy she looked. *Well, I do feel relaxed and I'm definitely having a good time,* Annabelle admitted. She felt as if a dark cloud had been lifted from her and gave a silent thanks that Bradley had come into her life. *And as long as I don't start thinking about him as a permanent fixture everything is going to be fine,* she cautioned herself.

Bradley leaned back in his seat and closed his eyes. He was tired. He and Annabelle had been pretty active these past two days. Being married to her had turned out to be very different from what he'd expected, he mused thoughtfully, but in a most pleasant way. He glanced at her. She was wearing a pair of tailored gray trousers with a double-breasted matching jacket over a silk blouse and gray four-inch high-heeled shoes. Her hair was pulled back and wound into a neat knot at the nape of her neck. All in all, she looked the part of the smartly attired executive on a business trip. She looked, in fact, a great deal like she had the first time he'd seen her. But this time, instead of seeing a cold, analytical woman, he pictured her the way she'd looked only a few hours earlier lying in bed beside him, wearing only a lacy little something he was busy taking off, her hair in total disarray, her mouth smiling.

Bradley drew a steadying breath. As tired as he was, he wished he could get her alone right this minute. *You're acting like a teenager on the make for the first time,* he admonished himself. *Go to sleep, you need the rest,* he added, and he closed his eyes once again.

Marriage can seriously hamper a man's concentration, he thought dryly several days later. He and Annabelle were in the living room of their hotel suite going over the final draft of the report they'd compiled. She was a quick study, and because of that, this job had gone swiftly.

Annabelle was still dressed in the tailored business suit she'd worn that day, and the desire to rid her of it was growing stronger by the moment. The fact that she was pacing the floor in front of him while she read wasn't helping. Instead of keeping his eyes focused on his copy of the report, his gaze kept shifting to the gentle swing of her hips. At last he tossed the report aside and rose. Blocking her path, he took her report and tossed it onto the couch with his; then he reached around her and began unfastening her hair.

A mischievousness sparkled in Annabelle's eyes. "I distinctly remember you telling me that you wanted to get this report done tonight," she said, mock reprimand in her voice.

"We'll get it done," he assured her, finishing with her hair and easing off her jacket. "But right this moment I'm having a very difficult time keeping my mind on business."

Annabelle experienced a surge of womanly power. "I suppose a break wouldn't do any harm," she conceded, her blood already beginning to race.

Bradley discarded her jacket then began unbuttoning her blouse. "I feel certain a break would do us both a world of good."

Annabelle loosened his tie, then removed it and tossed it onto the chair with her jacket. "They do say employees are more efficient and produce a higher quality of work if they take time to relax every once in a while."

"I mention that many times in my reports," he said, easing the blouse off her shoulders, then kissing the exposed flesh.

Annabelle laughed happily, then forgot about conversing as he claimed her mouth.

Later, sitting in bed trying to read the report, Bradley's mind again wandered to the woman beside him. She was wearing nothing but the sheet, which was pulled up to just above her breasts, then tucked around her. Her hair hung loose and was mussed from their lovemaking. She was chewing on a pencil while she read through her copy. He didn't think he'd ever seen a woman look more appealing.

"I was thinking that when this job is over, we'd go to my place in the Rockies," he suddenly heard himself saying. His gaze immediately shifted to his report. He'd never planned on taking Annabelle there. What he had planned to do was use his home in the Rockies as a private retreat when he needed time away from their marriage. When they weren't on assignment, he'd thought they would live in her home.

He couldn't justify this invitation even by telling himself that it was necessary for the running of his business, because it wasn't. He maintained a small office in Rock Springs, Wyoming, the nearest reasonable-sized town to his cabin. There he employed a secretary by the name of Mildred Gryst. Mildred was in her fifties, had a sharp, efficient mind, was scrupulously honest and totally reliable. She went through his mail and kept him apprised of all job offers and answered inquiries from possible clients. She also acted as his bookkeeper and all-round girl Friday. It was a simple but effective arrangement that allowed him to conduct his business from wherever he happened to be.

Annabelle glanced at him. The invitation had surprised her. She'd wondered if he was going to invite her to his home. His mother had mentioned that she and his father had been there only once. "I think of it as his hermit's cave," she'd told Annabelle. "It's a place he goes when he wants to get away from the rest of the world and he's welcome to it. It's much too isolated for me. But he loves it...."

Annabelle chewed on the inside of her bottom lip. So she was being invited to the hermit's cave. "Sounds like fun," she said noncommittally. But inside, she was excited. Careful, she cautioned herself. Remember that this arrangement is only temporary.

Bradley nodded, keeping his attention on the paper in front of him. But the printed words weren't registering. He'd invited Annabelle Royd—Annabelle Franklin, he corrected himself again. Anyway, he'd invited the woman beside him deeper into his life. Well, she *was* his wife, he reminded himself. It would only be natural for her to go to his home. Ignoring the sudden uneasiness he felt, he forced his mind back to the report.

A few days later Annabelle found herself at Bradley's mountain retreat. They'd flown into Rock Springs earlier that day. She'd met Mildred, then she and Bradley had picked up Bradley's Jeep, which was housed in the garage behind the office, and driven up to his home.

His mother had been right about its isolation. Annabelle guessed it had cost Bradley quite a bit to have phone lines and power lines run to the property.

It was definitely not what one could consider on the main road to anywhere.

It was a pretty house, though. It was an A-frame made of cedar set in a forest with a small mountain stream flowing past. And inside were all the conveniences of home. Also, like the Swynites' cabin, Bradley had his own generator in case the power was cut off during bad weather. He also had a housekeeper who came in regularly to make certain the place was kept fresh and ready for occupancy at a moment's notice.

Annabelle stood looking out the windowed back wall at the stream. It was late March now, but here the winter was still in full force. Behind her, Bradley was getting a fire started in the fireplace.

"It's beautiful up here," she said.

Bradley smiled, greatly pleased that she liked it. He swung his gaze to her. Even in the tailored business suit she'd worn for the trip, she looked as if she belonged in this place. Careful, he cautioned himself. Where Annabelle was concerned, he'd discovered that looks could be deceiving.

During the next few days, as they hiked, sat around the fire in the evenings reading and did all those domestic things he thought of married couples as doing, he found himself beginning to think that she actually might fit into the life he wanted. She honestly seemed to enjoy the solitude. And he definitely enjoyed being here with her.

However, all good things must come to an end, he thought regretfully as they sat down to dinner on a

Saturday evening two and a half weeks after their arrival. "Mildred sent me the information for the newest consulting job I've taken," he said.

Annabelle smiled at him. "As much as I've enjoyed being here," she said, "I have to admit I'm looking forward to getting back to work."

Bradley experienced a surge of disappointment. He had to confess that he felt the same way, but he'd been hoping that Annabelle wouldn't. *Idiot,* he chided himself. She was a career woman. She loved her work. He shouldn't have expected her to change. And why should she? She was very good at what she did. But she'd never be the wife he wanted. Admittedly he'd found himself creating a new image of her during the past days. It had her sitting in a rocking chair beside the fire crocheting while two babies played in a crib nearby. That image now vanished in a puff of smoke. "We'll fly out Sunday night. I've arranged for a meeting early Monday morning," he said, then began going over the details of the job with her.

There was something invigorating about putting her mind to a new task, Annabelle thought, picking out various points and asking him to elaborate. And she enjoyed working with Bradley. Life, she decided, was a lot more fun than she'd ever believed it could be.

The next morning, though, she was forced to reevaluate this statement. It had been very subtle, but she'd noticed a definite change in Bradley since the evening before. They'd developed a comfortable, congenial relationship during the past couple of weeks. But now it was as if he was attempting to put distance between them again. It wasn't blatant, he was still an ardent lover, but his smile wasn't as quick and didn't always reach his eyes.

Standing where she'd been standing the day they'd arrived, she gazed out the window. There was a deer who came to drink from the stream each afternoon. She'd grown fond of watching him. The thought that she might never see him again caused a sharp jab of pain. But she was beginning to think that Bradley would not invite her back.

It suddenly occurred to her that he might be worried that she was considering making this arrangement permanent. Her chin trembled slightly. The truth was, she wouldn't mind remaining his wife. But that wasn't what they'd agreed to.

"I was thinking," she said, turning toward him, "that it would be a good idea to set a date for the ending of this marriage. It's the practical thing to do. That way we can plan in advance when we should begin to show signs of not getting along."

Bradley laughed inwardly at himself. His ego was bigger than he'd thought. While he'd been considering keeping her as his wife, she was planning the divorce. "Getting bored with me already?" he asked.

Annabelle looked at him questioningly. Maybe he wasn't so eager to get rid of her, after all. She felt a bud of hope.

That was a stupid thing to say, Bradley berated himself. She was right. It would be best to set a date. "Just a bit of male egotism coming out," he said with a touch of self-mockery.

The hope died. "Your ego shouldn't feel damaged," she replied. "I guess I'm just trying to reassure you that I plan to live up to my end of the bargain. I'm very grateful to you. I don't want you to worry about being stuck with me."

"A man could do worse," Bradley heard himself admitting.

There was an edge in his voice that caused her to regard him narrowly. Once again the bud of hope threatened to bloom.

She's not what you want, Bradley reminded himself curtly. The thought of her with another man caused him an uncomfortable twinge, but he ignored it. "I'm sure you'll find your Mr. Right," he added.

But he's not you, Annabelle silently finished for him as hope died a final death. "I'm sure I will," she replied firmly. "How does two years from today as the date for the end of our marriage sound to you?"

"Sounds fine." It didn't really, he admitted, finding himself not looking at all forward to the end of this marriage. Then he berated himself. He couldn't honestly want this to linger on. He needed to get on with his life, find the wife he wanted.

"Good," she said. Now that an actual date was set, she wouldn't have any fantasies about this marriage lasting, she told herself. *And I can begin planning the rest of my life.*

But finding Mr. Right wasn't going to be easy, she mused a few days later. She and Bradley were having a quiet dinner in their hotel suite. Eating absently, she reviewed the available males she'd come into contact with since leaving Bradley's cabin. There were several she was working with on this latest job. But none of them had captured her interest. Well, it had taken several years before Bradley had stepped into her line of vision, she reminded herself. The thought that she might never meet anyone else like him occurred to her. Her jaw tensed. She would meet someone even better, she assured herself. She would meet someone who would love her.

Bradley was watching her. During the past few days, he'd noticed her covertly studying her male co-workers. Her interest in the other men irked him. He told himself that this agitation was merely caused by his ego and ordered himself not to pay any attention. After all, she would be free in a couple of years. But the thought nagged at him that while she was sitting across from him, she might be thinking about being with another man, possibly even *wanting* to be with another man. *You want her to be happy. You want her to find her Mr. Right,* he admonished himself. *But not while she's still married to me,* came the retort.

"I hope you realize that I expect the same fidelity from you that you require of me," he said, breaking the silence between them.

Annabelle looked up at him in surprise. "Of course."

She looked so incredibly innocent, he felt like a fool—a jealous fool, he corrected. Attempting to cover his embarrassment, he said with schooled indifference, "I've noticed you taking inventory of the unmarried men. I can't fault you for wanting to get on with your life. I'd like to get on with mine, too. If I thought it would look acceptable, I'd be willing for this marriage to end sooner than we stipulated, but I'm afraid that would cause the gossip we've been trying to avoid.''

For one brief moment, Annabelle had thought he might be jealous. But he'd just made it clear that he was only concerned about their reputations. Well, so was she!

''I was merely window-shopping for future possibilities,'' she said. ''After all the trouble we've gone through to make this facade look real, I wouldn't do anything to jeopardize it.''

Drop the subject, Bradley ordered himself, but instead he asked coolly, ''Find anything interesting?''

Annabelle shrugged. ''Nothing so far.''

Bradley experienced a surge of pleasure. That's not fair, he admonished himself. ''I'm sure you'll find your Mr. Right,'' he said encouragingly.

His patronizing manner grated. Annabelle told herself to be quiet, but instead, she heard herself saying, ''I'm curious. How do you plan to go about finding your Miss Right? Are you going to haunt the halls of the home-economics department at your local college?'' Her mouth formed a thoughtful pout. ''Or I suppose you could join several churches and alternate attendance so that you would have a larger number of available females to peruse.'' Immediately she dropped her gaze to her food. That had sounded definitely catty.

''I haven't really thought about it. However, those are possibilities,'' Bradley replied, mildly irritated that she could be so flippant about his search for a wife.

You're the one who's been so adamant about the kind of wife you want, he reminded himself. And he had been the one to bring up the subject of their future mates. In his mind's eye he saw himself leaning against the wall in a college hall. This was followed by a vision of him sitting alone in a church pew. Neither appealed to him.

The thought of Bradley with a new bride caused the food Annabelle was eating to taste like sawdust. *He's a good man; he deserves to have what he wants out of life.* "I hope you find what you're looking for," she said honestly.

Bradley raised his water glass. "May both our searches be successful."

Annabelle clinked her glass to his. "To our perfect mates." The thought that he was about as perfect as she was ever going to find crossed Annabelle's mind. Quickly she discarded it. He was not available to her. And he wasn't perfect, because he didn't love her. And with any luck, she thought, she'd find he had habits that drove her up a wall.

Two months later, she was still searching for one of those habits. Granted he had one or two little quirks she found slightly irritating, such as rattling his keys in his pocket when he was agitated and leaving the top off the toothpaste tube. But there was nothing that grated on her nerves, she admitted grudgingly as she massaged his shoulders one evening while he sat at his computer in their hotel room putting together a final report on a job they'd just completed here in Los Angeles. And he'd been generous with her about money.

More than generous. He'd arranged for her to receive a salary greater than what she'd been receiving at Swynite Industries. And all of it was being deposited in various investments in her name alone. He'd insisted that she live on the money in his accounts so that she would have a nice little nest egg when they parted. This made her feel sort of like a kept woman, and it also added a subtle impersonal air to their relationship. Just another little signal to be sure I don't forget this isn't permanent, she mused.

Bradley drew a deep breath. "You have great hands," he said.

"So do you," she replied.

Bradley smiled, the report instantly forgotten. "You think so?" he questioned playfully.

Annabelle knew immediately where this was leading, and an excitement was already stirring in her. She'd hoped that his lovemaking would have become at least a bit boring by now. But instead, she craved it even more. "I thought you wanted to finish that report tonight," she said with exaggerated mock innocence.

"A ten-minute break won't throw me that far off schedule," he returned flippantly.

She scowled. "Ten minutes?"

He grinned. "Half an hour."

"That's more like it," she replied, returning his grin. As they headed toward the bedroom, it occurred to her that they'd adapted very well to each other. They'd grown to know and respect each other's moods. And they definitely knew how to please each other.

Bradley had been certain that by now he would have become at least a little tired of Annabelle's company. But the opposite had happened. Each time they made love was as exciting as the last. Not only that, he honestly enjoyed working with her. She was bright and had a sense of humor that matched his. Earlier that evening he'd ordered himself to show some resistance to her, but just her impersonal massaging of his shoulders had kindled desire.

So much for my self-control, he chided himself as they reached the bedroom and he began to undress her. *Oh, well, a little healthy exercise is good for the mind and the body,* he reasoned philosophically.

Later as he again sat in front of his computer, he couldn't get Annabelle out of his mind. That had been happening a great deal lately and he wasn't happy about it. *My reactions to her are based on lust and ego,* he assured himself. What man wouldn't enjoy a woman who so openly enjoyed him? That was a sure way to stroke a man's ego.

He raked a hand agitatedly through his hair. His Annie was proving to be very dangerous to his peace of mind. "She's not *my* Annie," he growled under his breath. He raked both hands through his hair. He needed to put some time and distance between himself and her.

"Do you have a headache?"

He glanced up to see her entering the room. She was dressed in jeans and an old sweater and her hair was held loosely back with a bandanna. She looked exactly like the woman he'd been searching for all his life. In his mind, he pictured a baby left behind in the bedroom, sleeping peacefully.

Annabelle picked up her copy of the report and frowned down at it. "I think we need to rework the opening," she said, already scribbling in some new phrasing.

The homey vision vanished. *I definitely need some time on my own,* he decided. "I've been thinking," he said. "You've learned well. I'm considering a contract from a company in Atlanta, and there's another interesting one from a place in Florida. I think it's time you went out on your own. How about if you take the job in Atlanta? I'll take the one in Florida. If you run into any snags, I can fly up there and help you through them."

Annabelle's stomach knotted. She'd known that eventually he'd get bored with having her constantly around, but she'd hoped that when the time came, she'd be as tired of him as he was of her. She schooled her expression into one of enthusiasm. "Sounds like fun."

Bradley felt an uncomfortable nudge deep inside and was forced to admit that he'd thought she might show a little regret that they wouldn't be working together. *You can't have your cake and eat it, too,* he chided himself. "Guess you're anxious to try your wings," he said aloud.

"We career types are an independent breed," she replied, refusing to allow him to guess she would miss him. After all, she did have her pride.

Bradley nodded. This was the smartest move he'd made since this business had begun, he told himself.

Still, he discovered he wasn't quite ready to give up her company immediately. What harm could a few more days make, anyway? "We should be finished with this job by Thursday. That leaves us free until Sunday before we have to catch our flights east. How about if we spend Friday and Saturday sight-seeing and lounging around in San Francisco?"

Annabelle gave what she hoped was an indifferent shrug. "Sure. I've always wanted to see San Francisco."

But later that night, lying quietly beside him while he slept, she had second thoughts. He'd been good to her and he'd been honest with her. For her part, she'd constantly reminded herself of their bargain. The problem was that her heart hadn't been as easy to control as her mind. She remembered the way he smiled crookedly at her bad jokes. Then there was the gentleness and the control he'd shown on their wedding night. That was followed by memories of the passion they'd shared. There had also been quiet times when she'd simply enjoyed just sitting in the same room with him, reading or watching television. And she enjoyed working with him. Hot tears burned at the back of her eyes. She'd fallen in love with him. She'd spent a lot of time telling herself that the attraction was only physical, but that was a lie and she knew it.

And you knew the time would come when he'd want you around less often, she scolded herself. She just hadn't expected it to come so soon. But now it had, and she was having a very difficult time facing it. If she went to San Francisco, there was the possibility that she might make a fool of herself or embarrass him by letting him guess her true feelings. Even worse, he might feel guilty, and she didn't want that. Her jaw firmed as she made up her mind about what she had to do.

The next morning at breakfast, she said with practiced indifference, "The trip to San Francisco sounds like fun, but I really think you should go without me. I need to go back to Pittsburgh and check on my home. Linda hinted that the triplets might forget what I look like if I don't come visit soon."

There, she'd said it. Her breath seemed to lock in her lungs and she realized she was hoping he would attempt to change her mind or volunteer to go back to Pittsburgh with her. She knew it was a foolish wish. Even if he did, it wouldn't be because he'd learned to care deeply for her. It would merely mean that he wasn't entirely bored with her company yet.

That she seemed almost anxious to get away from him bothered Bradley. Well, wasn't getting away from her what he wanted? he questioned himself. Yes, it was, came his firm response. Aloud he said, "You go on to Pittsburgh. And I'll fly to Rock Springs. I should check in with Mildred, anyway, and make certain everything is fine at my place."

Annabelle nodded. Though she'd known he wasn't going to invite her back to his mountain retreat, still it hurt. Suddenly she wanted to be totally free from this marriage.

"I've been thinking about what you said about our marriage ending too quickly and causing gossip," she said. "But it occurs to me that with us being two high-powered executive types, no one would be surprised if we began to clash quickly. And I'm always hearing about marriages that don't even survive the first month. Maybe we should consider this the beginning of the end. For the next few months we can work separately, but maintain the pretense of keeping our marriage going. Then after about five months, we could announce that we have irreconcilable differences and apply for a divorce. That way we can both get on with our lives."

For a moment Bradley considered rejecting her idea. Then he mentally laughed at this impulse. Hadn't he been telling himself that getting on with his life was exactly what he wanted to do? And clearly it was what Annabelle wanted.

"I agree," he replied.

Chapter Eleven

Annabelle arrived home in Pittsburgh late on Friday night. She'd planned a late arrival because she wanted some time alone before facing Linda and Frank.

After a hot shower, she dressed in an old cotton gown, then went downstairs. She was too restless to sleep. She'd hoped that being back among her own things would help erase the memories of Bradley. What she hadn't counted on was remembering the times they'd spent here. As she passed through the living room, she recalled a particularly lively chase that had ended very pleasantly.

The hot tears she'd refused to shed before again burned at the back of her eyes. *It's silly to cry over something you knew was going to happen,* she scolded herself.

Entering the kitchen, she saw a pie sitting in the middle of her kitchen table. Next to it was a note from Linda that read:

Dear Ann,
Welcome home. We've missed you. I even baked your favorite pie—apple with raisins and walnuts. Hope you enjoy it. I'll expect you for dinner Saturday. If Bradley was able to change his plans and accompany you, then he's invited, too. I'd like to spend some more time with that handsome new brother-in-law of mine.

                                        Love,
                                        Linda

"Soon to be *ex*-brother-in-law," Annabelle said with quiet resignation. Suddenly the dam burst and the tears flowed in rivers down her cheeks.

When the tears finally slowed, she poured herself a glass of milk and cut herself a piece of the pie. Glancing at the clock, she noted that it was two in the morning. "A woman should be allowed to indulge herself when her marriage comes to an end," she muttered, sitting down and beginning to eat.

While Annabelle sat eating her pie, Bradley was standing, his back stiff, staring out his living-room window. Outside, only the moon and stars gave illumination to the dark landscape. Inside, his only light came from the fire in the hearth. He'd stood alone like this a thousand times before and found a peace with the world. But tonight he could find no peace. Instead, an incredible loneliness pervaded him.

Annabelle's image entered his mind. He tried to concentrate on her in her business suit, but the picture blurred and when it emerged again she was in her jeans and sweater, and playing with Linda's triplets. He blinked his eyes and forced her back into her business suit. But instead of the staid expression of a stern businesswoman, she was smiling that half amused, half I-can't-believe-you-said-that smile she used when he'd made a particularly awful pun. He drew a tired breath. And then there was the way she wrinkled her nose when she was working on something she knew wasn't quite right but didn't know how to fix it.

"You came up here to put her out of your mind," he growled.

He ordered himself to think of the kind of woman he'd always pictured sharing his life. Before he'd met Annabelle, she'd had no particular appearance— whether she was blond, brunette or red-haired had depended on the mood he was in. Tonight, however, she looked like Annabelle. He scowled. Then he thought of the two children—the boy and girl. They were at the toddler stage, happily playing in the center of the room. Suddenly they were dressed in little business suits, and their toys had become computers.

The scowl on his face deepened as resolve etched itself into his features. He knew what he wanted and he was a man who achieved his goals.

Annabelle slept late Saturday morning. When she did finally awake, she lay in bed for a long time. "You just don't want to face Linda and Frank, do you?'' she muttered. ''Well, you can't stay in here all day.''

Tossing the covers aside, she ordered herself to her feet. By noon she was dressed and sitting in her kitchen eating another piece of pie.

The ringing of the phone interrupted her.

''I wanted to call earlier, but just in case Bradley came with you, I didn't want to interrupt any morning *activities,*'' Linda said when Annabelle answered.

Annabelle experienced a sharp jab of pain when Linda's exaggerated playful way of saying ''activities'' made it clear she was referring to lovemaking. Actually, what had occurred between her and Bradley had never been lovemaking, Annabelle corrected, at least not on Bradley's part. It had been two people physically enjoying one another. ''You wouldn't have interrupted anything,'' she assured her sister levelly. ''Bradley didn't come with me.''

There was a brief silence on the other end of the line, then Linda said sharply, ''Something's wrong. I can tell. I'm on my way over.''

Before Annabelle could protest, the line went dead. A couple of minutes later, Linda entered through the back door. As she crossed the kitchen to join her sister at the table, her gaze fell pointedly on the pie. ''You've eaten three-quarters,'' she said, the concern in her voice deepening.

Annabelle shrugged. ''It's a great pie. Your best ever.''

''It is not inconceivable for me to devour half a pie on my own just because it tastes good,'' Linda said, patting her hips to imply they were a little more am-

ple than she would like. "But you never indulge
yourself like this unless something has really upset
you." Her gaze narrowed. "Have you and Bradley had
a fight?"

The time had come to tell Linda the truth, Annabelle decided. But as the words formed in her mind,
tears welled in her eyes, and she knew that if she
started talking about Bradley, she was going to begin
sobbing all over again. She felt like an idiot. What
self-respecting woman would bawl over a man who
had never professed to love her, who had made it clear
from the beginning that she was not what he wanted
in a wife? She wanted to tell Linda the truth, but she
wanted to do it with some dignity, not blubbering like
a lovesick fool. She swallowed back the explanation.
Later today she would tell her sister everything, but
not right now. At the moment, all she could bring
herself to say was, "The marriage isn't working out
the way we'd hoped."

"All couples have trouble adjusting," Linda replied philosophically. "I'm sure you'll work it out."
She assumed the look of one about to impart some
very shrewd advice. "However, you cannot work it
out separately. You've got to work it out together."

A lump that felt as large as a baseball formed in
Annabelle's throat as she recalled that Bradley hadn't
seemed to be able to get rid of her fast enough. As
clearly as if he was standing in front of her, she could
visualize the relief that had been on his face when he'd
said goodbye to her at the airport.

"Right now each of us just needs a little time on our
own," she replied, forking another bite of pie. She

would never regret having married him. But she did wish this part didn't hurt so much.

"I think you're wrong about that," Linda argued. "Speaking from my experience, you should call him, or better still, go be with him."

If she thought he would be happy to see her, Annabelle would have been on her way to the airport in a second. But she knew he wouldn't. The urge to sob was growing stronger. "How about a piece of pie?" she offered, attempting to change the subject. "And you haven't told me a thing about the triplets. Has Jack started talking, or are his sisters still chattering so incessantly that he hasn't had a chance to get a word in edgewise?"

Linda frowned at her. "Avoiding a problem never makes it go away."

"You're right." Annabelle breathed a tired sigh. And waiting until later wasn't going to make talking about Bradley any easier. Even if it meant getting the story out between sobs, she had to tell Linda the truth. Maybe it would even help. She was willing to try anything to relieve some of this hurt. "There is something I have to tell you," she said. "My marriage—"

The ringing of the front doorbell interrupted her.

"Aren't you going to answer that?" Linda asked when Annabelle simply groaned, fell silent and remained seated.

"No." Annabelle concentrated on what had been a huge slice of pie but was almost all eaten now. "I can't face anyone but you at the moment." She screwed her face into a self-conscious grimace. "My stomach is beginning to hurt."

"That," Linda replied, "doesn't surprise me."

The doorbell rang again.

Linda started toward the hall. "I'll answer it, get rid of whoever is there, and then we'll talk," she said over her shoulder.

"I'm behaving ridiculously," Annabelle scolded herself when she was alone. "I've got to get a grip on my emotions. This is supposed to be a new beginning, not an end."

"Frank has come up with some unique ways of making up when we've had an argument," Linda said as she returned to the kitchen. She paused in the doorway, an amused smile spreading across her face. "But Bradley has definitely outdone him."

Annabelle frowned in confusion. The frown deepened when she heard the sound of clanking metal coming from behind her sister. Then Linda stepped aside and Bradley entered. He was dressed in full armor.

Annabelle gasped.

"I think it's time for me to leave," Linda said, making a quick exit out the back door.

Annabelle barely noticed her departure. She was watching Bradley. Don't jump to any conclusions, she cautioned herself.

"You once said you wanted to marry a knight in shining armor," he said gruffly. "I'm not as perfect as my namesake, but I'd like to be that knight."

Annabelle's throat constricted. She could have sworn from the way he'd said it that he meant it as a real proposal. Don't start believing what you want to believe, she warned herself. "Are you talking about two years, or a lifetime?"

"I was thinking in terms of a lifetime," he replied. A warm plea entered his eyes. "I know that's not what we agreed on. But I want a chance to convince you that I'm worth falling in love with."

Joy spread through Annabelle. "I thought you wanted a more domestically-minded woman," she said shakily, almost afraid to believe what he was saying.

"I did, too," Bradley confessed. "From the time I was a kid and used to come home from school and find my mother baking cookies, I pictured myself married to a woman whose only concern was our home and family." He looked sheepish. "What I hadn't planned on was you coming into my life. When I first saw you, I thought you were the epitome of the cool businesswoman. You were exactly the kind of woman I told myself I would never want for a wife, the kind of female I would never even consider dating. Then I came here and found you with Linda's triplets." Frustration shone in his eyes. "The more I got to know you, the more you threatened my peace of mind. After that weekend in the cabin, I decided that it would be best if I kept my distance. Then the Swynites pulled their little stunt, and we ended up married."

He took a step toward her, his armor clanking as he moved. "I thought marriage to you would cure me of the fascination I had begun to feel for you. But instead, I discovered I enjoyed your company, your humor, your gentleness. I also admired your business talent. I was finally forced to admit that I was falling in love with you.''

His words caused a rush of happiness, but it was quickly dampened by a wariness. She knew that the pain she'd been going through these past couple of days was nothing compared to the pain she'd go through if she let herself freely love him, then discovered that they couldn't make their marriage work. ''I can't be the kind of wife you pictured yourself as having,'' she said, determined to make this point clear.

''I know,'' he replied. ''And I would never ask you to even try. You're the kind of woman who enjoys having a career. It makes you happy and your happiness is what matters most to me. You please me just the way you are. I was wrong about the wife I thought I wanted. I like having you working beside me. Other couples have their careers and their families, too. I don't see any reason we can't.'' The plea returned to his eyes. ''Will you give me a chance to prove I can be the husband *you* want?''

Annabelle's heart was pounding wildly. A happiness she had thought she would never feel filled her. ''I suppose I could fall in love with you,'' she said. An admiring grin spread over her face. ''You do look rather handsome in that armor.''

He smiled back and her heart lurched. A warmth filled her. She rose from the table and moved toward him. ''Of course, you also look rather good out of it.''

His smile broadened. ''I'll need some help. I couldn't even drive in this getup. I had to leave my car at the costume shop and hire a taxi to get here.''

Annabelle's mouth formed a playful pout. "Well, I certainly don't want your actions inhibited. Especially if you were intending to begin your persuasive maneuvers right away." She glanced over her shoulder at the mostly eaten apple pie. "I could use some exercise."

He bowed clumsily. "I am at my lady's command."

"In that case..." She let the rest of the sentence trail off as she began helping him out of the armor.

Quite a while later, Annabelle lay quietly in Bradley's arms. She'd always enjoyed his company in bed, but this time had been the most exciting yet. This time they'd truly made love. She felt relaxed and happy and at peace with the world.

"Annie," Bradley said, shifting so that he was on his side, looking down at her, "I need to know that there's a chance you could learn to love me. I know I can please you in bed, but I want to have more than just a physical relationship with you. I want to really be your knight in shining armor."

That he actually sounded worried surprised her. "You are," she assured him. "And I do love you."

Bradley smiled, then a questioning look spread over his face. "Does anyone make tailored suits for toddlers?"

Annabelle frowned up at him. "I suppose someone does. But that doesn't sound very comfortable for the child or very practical. Why?"

He grinned. "Just a thought."

Annabelle shook her head as if questioning his sanity. Then his questions were forgotten as her passion was rekindled. Slowly, enjoying the feel of him beneath her palms, she ran her hands over his chest and up around his neck.

Her touch sparked desire. As he drew her into his arms, he had a sudden vision of himself and Annie and two children, a boy and a girl, all dressed in blue pin-striped suits. It was a perfect family portrait, he thought.

*   *   *   *   *

COMING NEXT MONTH

#886 A CHANGED MAN—Karen Leabo *Written in the Stars*
Conservative Virgo man Stephen Whitfield was too uptight for
impulsive Sagittarius Jill Ballantine. But Jill sensed a lovable man
beneath that stuffy accountant exterior. All Stephen needed was a
little loosening up!

#887 WILD STREAK—Pat Tracy
Erin Clay had always been off-limits to Linc Severance—first as his
best friend's wife and then as his best friend's widow. Now Linc was
back in town . . . and ready to test the forbidden waters.

#888 YOU MADE ME LOVE YOU—Jayne Addison
Nothing Caroline Phelps ever did seemed to turn out right—*except*
meeting sexy Jack Corey. But when life's little disasters began to
occur, could Caroline trust Jack to always be there?

#889 JUST ONE OF THE GUYS—Jude Randal
Dana Morgan was a do-it-yourself woman—more at home in a
hardware store than in a beauty parlor. But Spencer Willis was out to
prove there *was* one thing Dana couldn't do alone . . . fall in love!

#890 MOLLY MEETS HER MATCH—Val Whisenand
To Molly Evans, Brian Forrester was a gorgeous male specimen. So
what if he was in a wheelchair? But she *couldn't* ignore his stubborn
pride—or his passion . . . even if she wanted to.

#891 THE IDEAL WIFE—Joleen Daniels
Sloan Burdett wanted Lacey Sue Talbert like no woman on earth, but
if he was going to have her, he'd have to move fast. Lacey Sue was
about to walk down the aisle with his brother. . . .

AVAILABLE THIS MONTH:

#880 BABY SWAP
Suzanne Carey

#881 THE WIFE HE WANTED
Elizabeth August

**#882 HOME IS WHERE THE
HEART IS**
Carol Grace

**#883 LAST CHANCE FOR
MARRIAGE**
Sandra Paul

#884 FIRE AND SPICE
Carla Cassidy

**#885 A HOLIDAY TO
REMEMBER**
Brittany Young

Love has a language all its own, and for centuries, flowers have symbolized love's finest expression. Discover the language of flowers—and love—in this romantic collection of 48 favorite books by bestselling author Nora Roberts.

Two titles are available each month at your favorite retail outlet.

In August, look for:

Tempting Fate, **Volume #13**
From this Day, **Volume #14**

In September, look for:

All the Possibilities, **Volume #15**
The Heart's Victory, **Volume #16**

Collect all 48 titles
and become fluent in

Silhouette
R O M A N C E™

★ WRITTEN IN THE STARS ★

WHEN A VIRGO MAN MEETS A SAGITTARIUS WOMAN

Accountant Stephen Whitfield's aunt was being swindled and it was all Jill Ballantine's fault! Straitlaced Stephen had never been able to get along with his free-spirited cousin by marriage— she'd always known how to make him lose control. But now Jill wanted Stephen to lose his heart...to her! There's a cosmic attraction in Karen Leabo's A CHANGED MAN, coming in September, only from Silhouette Romance. It's WRITTEN IN THE STARS!